D0454852

No Longer Property of
ANYTHINK LIBRARIES/
RANGEVIEW LIBRARY DISTRICT

Together at Midnight

ALSO BY JENNIFER CASTLE

The Beginning of After

You Look Different in Real Life

What Happens Now

Together at Midnight

JENNIFER CASTLE

HARPER TEEN
An Imprint of HarperCollinsPublishers

HarperTeen is an imprint of HarperCollins Publishers.

Together at Midnight
Copyright © 2018 by Jennifer Castle
All rights reserved. Printed in the United States of America.
No part of this book may be used or reproduced in any manner whatsoever without written
permission except in the case of brief quotations embodied in critical articles and reviews. For
information address HarperCollins Children's Books, a division of HarperCollins Publishers, 195
Broadway, New York, NY 10007.
www.epicreads.com

ISBN 978-0-06-225051-3

17 18 19 20 21 PC/LSCH 10 9 8 7 6 5 4 3 2 1

First Edition

For Kathleen Spring,
who made it look easy

Together at Midnight

DECEMBER 26

Kendall

HERE NOW, A LIST:

THINGS TO DO TO MAKE NEXT YEAR PERFECT

Okay, that's way too much pressure. I cross out *Perfect* and replace it with *Not Suck*, knowing full well that even *Not Suck* might be reaching for the stars.

1) Get completely ready to go back to Fitzpatrick.

I'm not sure how to accomplish "completely ready to go back," but writing it down feels like a first step. I've spent the last semester in a study abroad program and now I'm home. My high school is still here, right where I left it. It didn't, for instance, explode in a blaze of white-hot glory while I was gone. When the holiday break is over in seven days, I'll have to exist there again.

    2) Start your book. Then, for the love of all things holy,
        FINISH it.

My novel is about the end of the world, and so far I've come up with a title, *Together at Midnight*, and drawn sketches and written bios of all the main characters. Now I just need to begin the actual writing. That's the no-fun part, which is why I never do it, which is why I have to put it on a goddamn list.

    3) Achieve quality time with Ari.

My best friend. We haven't been apart this long, ever. We emailed back and forth a bit while I was away, but I need to know she still fits snugly into her spot in my life. Especially because now that spot has to accommodate her boyfriend. (Sigh.)

    4) Get in touch with Jamie.

I stare at those five too-simple words. Then I add:

Let him know I'm home. Set up a time to meet.

Still doesn't seem like enough so I add more:

Become a couple. Have a great spring together. Go to
    the prom. BE IN LOVE.

Nope. Dial it back, girl. I scratch that last part out.

I met Jamie last summer, when Ari and his friend Camden started dating. We clicked and I really liked him, until he told me he didn't think of me *that way*. Then, after I left for Europe, he emailed me one of his photos. I sent him one back. Over the last few months, we've been having the kind of correspondence that makes you obsessed with your inbox and you hate hate hate that but also, you love it.

There. A list that will either motivate me out of bed or drive me deeper under the covers. We shall see. But at least it's done what all my lists are intended to do: coax the Thought Worms in my head to wriggle out of hiding, whispering to them, *You don't need to bother Kendall anymore! Come play on this nice clean page!*

I put down the notebook and pencil and look around my room. During my time with the Movable School program, I went to Paris, Rome, and London, Saint-Tropez and Monaco, the green hills of Ireland and the white cliffs of Dover. Now I'm back within these pink-and-purple walls, staring at a poster of kittens eating cake. (The kittens are as cute as they were when I was eleven, but still.) How do I fit inside this space again?

There's another person in my house who knows what this feels like and might be able to tell me what to do about it, so I get up to find him.

On my way out of the room, I pat my enormous red suitcase on the shoulder. It sits just inside the door, only partially unzipped. For three days since I got back from Europe, it's dared me to unpack it, and for three days, I've wimped out of that dare.

My brother Emerson is sprawled across his bed as if someone threw him ten feet and this is how he landed. At first, I can't tell which blanket-lumps are which. I definitely don't want to touch his head and have it turn out not to be his head. I've made that mistake before. I watch him for a moment, parts of him hanging off the mattress because it's the same mattress he's had since he was twelve.

One of the lumps moves. Definitely his head. I reach out and flick it through the covers.

"Hey," I whisper.

My brother groans like an animal in pain. A woolly mammoth sinking into a tar pit.

"It's Kendall," I add.

"I know," says Emerson. "Strawberry shampoo."

"I have to ask you something."

"Ken, it's too early for one of your random questions."

"How do you stand coming back home?"

Em laugh-grunts. "Welcome to the rest of your life, kid."

"Be serious," I say, flicking him again. "I need to know before you leave."

He rolls over and pulls the covers down so I can see his face. Looking at him is like looking at myself, in the alternate timeline where I was born a boy. Same auburn hair, same awkward nose. But of course on him, it all works. Me, not so much.

"Sometimes I pretend I'm not actually in my body," says Emerson, "and the thinking and feeling part of me is hovering near the ceiling, watching all the action."

"Like the way people describe near-death experiences?"

"Try it sometime."

"What time did Andrew move?" I ask.

Andrew is Emerson's boyfriend. Even though they're both twenty-two and live together in Manhattan, and my parents have known Em was gay since he was thirteen and probably way before that, my dad's enforcing an "unmarried couples don't sleep together under my roof" rule. He says it was the same when my other two brothers brought girlfriends home to visit. He says changing the rules because Andrew and Emerson are both guys would be reverse discrimination, which is a good point none of us wanted to admit out loud.

Emerson gives me his best fake-innocent look, complete with big eyes, something I can't pull off even though we have almost the same face.

"Oh, come on," I say. "He came in right after Mom and Dad went to bed, right?"

Emerson laughs. "What can I say? I sleep better if he's here. He went back to the couch sometime early this morning. What time is it now?"

I glance at the clock above his bed. "Eight forty-five."

"Jesus!" he says, throwing back the covers. "We have a cab coming at nine to take us to the train. Can you see if Andrew's up?"

As Emerson starts frantically getting dressed, I rush downstairs. Past my brother Walker's room, where Walker will probably be asleep most of the day. I always get a two-second whiff of marijuana when I walk by and I think it's permanently embedded in the wood of his door. Then I pass my oldest brother Sullivan's door, shut tight and unopened for so long, I keep forgetting it's not a closet. He's not there because he and his wife are staying at a hotel for this Christmas visit, which is one of the many reasons why being twenty-six sounds awesome.

Yup, we're Sullivan, Walker, Emerson, and Kendall. People joke that my dad was trying to create his own law firm, but my brothers are actually named after artists and writers my parents admire. I was the accident baby, aka the "I can't believe our parents are still having sex" baby. You'd think that after three boys, my mother would jump at the chance for a girl's name, something that ends with a *Y* or *A* sound and has *i*'s that can be dotted with hearts. But, no. Kendall was the last name of the teacher who inspired her to be a history professor. Thanks a lot, dude-who-died-right-before-I-was-born.

The door of my parents' room is always left open a crack so the cat can come and go. I see my dad asleep in bed, but not my mom.

Downstairs in the kitchen, Andrew's already making coffee. For the record, I really love Andrew.

"Hey, monkey," says Andrew. (I also love that he calls me this.) "Is he up?"

"Just now," I say. "Where's Mom?"

"She went out for a run but said she'll be back before our cab comes."

I nod. Of course she did. Janet Parisi doesn't let Christmas Day calories just sit there in her body, being useless.

Suddenly, the sound of a car horn makes us both jump.

Andrew glances out the window. "Good God. The cab's early."

"Dammit!" yells Emerson from upstairs. "It's early!"

Andrew sighs. "I'll go ask him to wait."

He pulls on his boots and coat, then grabs his neat little rolling suitcase and heads out the door. Painfully frigid air from the outside world rushes in. I watch him steer the suitcase down the icy path to the street. The cab driver hops out and pops the trunk, then takes Andrew's bag for him.

I watch myself running toward the cab and throwing open the door and leaping inside.

No, wait. That's only happening in my head.

I press my hand to the window and force myself to lay my whole palm against the cold, cold glass. This should keep me here, in reality.

Emerson jets down the stairs, a big leather satchel slung across his body, a shopping bag full of opened Christmas gifts in one hand. His hair, which is never rumpled, is rumpled.

"Why do you have to go back?" I ask him. "Andrew's the one who has to work. You have the week off."

Andrew writes for an online magazine. Emerson teaches sixth-grade science at a private school. They've been together since their sophomore year in college and it's all unbearably adorable.

He shakes his head. "I wish I could, but another night here is beyond the limits of my out-of-body coping mechanism."

Andrew comes back into the house. "Ready?"

Emerson takes the coffeepot off the burner, swigs some straight from the pot, then puts it down and wipes his mouth. "Ready."

"Your mom's not back from her run yet," says Andrew. "She'll be mad she didn't get to say good-bye."

"Eh, we're seeing her and Kendall in a few days when they come in to see *Wicked*."

Andrew takes Emerson's shopping bag from him and hands him his coat. Emerson turns to me. "I'm glad you're home, Ken. I'm glad you had an amazing time in Europe."

For some reason, this makes me want to weep.

"It was a good Christmas," I say, nodding, my hand still on the windowpane.

"See you on Wednesday."

I pull myself away from the window so Emerson and I can hug. Then I hug Andrew, and then they leave the house. As the door opens, the air lashes my face and it feels horrible but I also don't mind it because I'm having that flicker again.

This time, I picture myself sitting between Emerson and Andrew in the backseat of the cab.

Before I really understand what I'm doing, I step onto the porch and shout, "Wait!"

Holy crap, the cold through the soles of my feet in socks. Andrew, Emerson, and the cab driver all turn to me and I guess I'm supposed to follow that up with something.

So I yell, "Can I come with you?"

They both just stare, as blank as the snow between me and

them, until Emerson asks, "What do you mean?"

"Can I come stay with you guys? In the city? For a few days?"

Emerson steps gingerly back down the path toward me, not taking his eyes off my face. Does it show? How much I need to go with him?

"We have to leave right now or we'll miss the train," he says.

"Give me two minutes."

"Mom will be furious. And confused."

"I'll handle it."

"We do have a guest room now," adds Andrew, to Emerson. "It would be great to break it in."

Emerson sighs. Glances back and forth between Andrew and me. "Fine," he finally says, cracking a smile.

I dart into the house, up the stairs, into my room. Tuck my phone in the pocket of my pajama top. When I grab the handle of my suitcase, I can almost hear it hissing, *Yes!* To avoid making any noise, I pick the thing up. It's obscenely heavy. I could die this way.

I make it to the front door, pull on my long wool coat and my winter boots, then haul the suitcase outside.

"Oh, for God's sake," says Emerson when he sees it.

Within moments, the trunk is full and slammed shut and it's just as I pictured: I'm sandwiched between Emerson and Andrew on the way to the train station in Poughkeepsie.

This was totally not on the list.

Max

"LEAVE THAT ON CNN OR I'LL WRITE YOU OUT OF THE will!"

My grandfather's voice booms through the apartment. It woke me up. At first, I thought it was the voice of God, and let me tell you, that's a hell of a way to gain consciousness. Now I'm just lying in bed, listening to God be an asshole.

"That threat doesn't work anymore," I hear my dad say. "Can you come up with something a little less ridiculous?"

"Please, Big E," adds a high, tight voice. My aunt. Dad's sister. "The kids shouldn't be seeing all this refugee footage. They'll have nightmares for days. Just a half hour of Nickelodeon, okay? While we get everyone packed up?"

There's a noise like something being dropped. Or thrown. That poor remote. It has more duct tape on it than, well, a duct.

My grandfather, Ezra Levine, aka Big E to those of us forced to put up with him, is in fine form. He's got a heart condition, high blood pressure, and two bad hips, but his biggest ailment is chronic jerkiness. Always has been, but more so since my grandmother died in March. It's in honor of her, our Nanny, that we gathered at Big E's enormous Park Avenue apartment for Christmas. She was the Irish Catholic girl who made it magical for everyone. Especially her grumpy Jewish husband.

Everyone means my parents, my sister, my aunt and uncle, their two kids, and me. They stuck me in my dad's old room with my twin cousins, Theo and Ezra. I'm eighteen. They're four. It's like the world's smallest, weirdest overnight camp.

I can't wait to get back home. Back to work. Away from the glances of my extended family. Even the four-year-olds look at me like, *Tell me again why you're not at college right now?*

There's a knock.

"Max, it's Dad. Are you awake?"

"Yeah."

My dad comes in and looks around the room. The airplane wallpaper's still there from when he was little, along with a single faded poster of Freddie Mercury of Queen, shirtless in tight white pants, gripping a microphone. So yeah, it's a strange vibe.

Dad pulls out the small chair from the even smaller wooden desk. It's where he must have done many hours of elite private school homework. Then he takes a deep breath and stares at me. This feels ominous.

"It was a good Christmas," I say.

"It was. Considering."

"That Big E is being shitty to everyone?"

"Don't be disrespectful," says Dad, but then he laughs. "But okay, shitty is one word for it."

"Aunt Suze said his home aide quit."

"Yes. That's what we wanted to talk to you about."

I look around. Who's *we*? The look on Dad's face says it all: I'm not going to like what's coming next.

"Maxie," he continues. "We need a favor from you. It's a big one, but I know you're up to the task."

Oh, crap. He's going to ask me to help get my grandfather into the bathtub.

"Suze and I will hire a new aide," says Dad, "but it's going to take a few days to find someone. I need to go back to work tomorrow. Your aunt has to get the kids home to New Jersey."

The picture comes together. It involves much, much more than an old naked guy in a bathroom.

"Maxie, you're the only one of us who doesn't have commitments this week. . . ."

Go ahead, rub it in. I'm the moron who was all set to start at Brown and then at the last minute, just a week before freshman orientation, said, *Hey, can I take a rain check?*

One of my reasons for this was right. The other was wrong. Wrong enough to overshadow the right. To make me regret every day that I'm not in Providence, Rhode Island. They're holding my spot until next year, but I should be in that empty space now. Filling every corner of it. Letting it fill me in return.

"We need you . . . ," my dad continues. "No, we're asking you . . . to stay here until a new aide can start. We're talking maybe two days, tops. Someone has to be in the apartment, or at least nearby, in case he needs something."

"Big E and I . . . ," I start to say, but can't utter the rest of it. We have nothing to talk about. He thinks grandfathering means sending me magazine articles he wants me to read. I'm not sure he even likes me.

"I know," says Dad, and maybe he actually does. "Look, you won't be stuck in the apartment with him. You can go out, do your own thing. See a movie. Check out a museum. Just be in the area, in case he calls."

The truth is, I really don't have anything better to do at home. I've been working at a telemarketing company, trying to earn as much money as I can for college, but they gave everyone the week off. Plus, if I'm here, I can't hang out with my high school friends or see my ex-girlfriend, Eliza. That's all good.

"Sure, Dad," I finally say. "You're right. It should be me."

Dad claps me on the shoulder. "You're a great kid, Maxie. You always come through in a pinch."

I totally do. When someone needs something, I'm there.

But where am I when nobody needs anything? *Who* am I when nobody needs anything? That, my friends, is the question.

* * *

An hour later, both families are packed up and ready to hit the road.

Except me, of course. I've been sitting in the kitchen, nursing a giant cup of coffee. My sister, Allie, comes over and takes a swig. She's fifteen.

"Vaya con Dios, hermano," she says.

"Thanks."

Mom and Aunt Suze hug me in rapid succession. The little cousins hug me because Aunt Suze orders them to. My dad claps me on the shoulder again. Big E has fallen asleep in his recliner and I don't know what's louder, the TV or his snoring.

Aunt Suze takes me aside and runs down the list of his medications. "He knows what he has to take, and when. Just check in with him a couple times a day to make sure."

She's emptied the fridge of anything he's not supposed to eat. Now she hands me a stack of menus from nearby restaurants, with certain items circled. I can order his lunch and dinner from any of those selections. Then she gives me a list of phone numbers for his myriad doctors. "But if it's not an emergency, call me first," says Suze. "I can be here inside an hour."

I look at the frown line between her eyebrows and understand, for the first time, how much energy she pours into my grandfather. It must be like she's got three kids, not two. I'm overcome with sympathy and appreciation for her. Then, relief. That I can be useful.

Just like that, both families are gone. Nobody wanted to

wake Big E, so they never said good-bye to him. This might infuriate the guy, or maybe he couldn't care less. I watch him for a few moments, his chest rising and falling. There's so much heaviness to the movement. I know he's just a person. He's known me all my life. We share blood and a middle name.

I'm scared completely shitless.

Kendall

WE RAN TO CATCH THE SUBWAY HEADING UPTOWN to Emerson and Andrew's apartment, and I don't want to talk about how hard it was getting my suitcase through Grand Central. Now I'm recovering in a seat tucked against the wall. The guy sitting next to me wears Ray-Ban sunglasses, black fingerless gloves, and a leather jacket. He's reading a book in French and doesn't seem to care that a panting girl and her ginormous luggage are invading his personal space.

If he were a character in my novel, he'd be like Judd Nelson in *The Breakfast Club*, but also valedictorian of his class. Quiet and full of secrets. All the girls at his high school make fun, but secretly lust after him. One girl in particular is obsessed with his fingernails peeking out of those gloves, because they're always clean and polished.

This is a thing I do: turn real people into characters in whatever I'm writing. I draw a sketch of them, then jot down a few details. A name and where they live, what they do, what they want. Thought Worms that spring free from nowhere or everywhere.

The people-watching is one reason why I love riding the subway in New York. Also, I'm fascinated by how it can be loud and quiet at the same time. Outside the train, it sounds like universes are colliding and shattering, but here in the car almost nobody talks.

I check my phone. There's a recent text from Mom.

What time are you coming home from the city?

This is sticky. I answer **Staying overnight at Emerson's, will text later** because that's all the information I have for her, and also for me.

OK, she replies, and if a pair of typed letters can look pissed off, these do. I don't blame her. I've been gone four months and Mom was looking forward to some mom/daughter quality time, and here's proof that I'm awful.

She also knows what a stupid idea this is. What am I going to do in Manhattan? I have almost no spending money left. I came back from Europe with twenty-four dollars and also some random currency from different countries. Coins that don't feel the right weight, bills in strange colors, all with faces and names I don't recognize (except Queen Elizabeth, duh). If I'm desperate, I'll exchange them. But right now I just like to see them in my wallet because it feels like the rest of the world is waving to me.

I open up a photo album on my phone that has twenty-seven images in it. I remember when Jamie sent me each one, and where I was, and what I sent back in response. One picture is of a tree flush with bright red leaves, a clear blue sky backdrop. Another is a shot of two tip jars at a coffeehouse where one says "Invisibility" and one says "Flight," and the Invisibility jar was winning.

Jamie never wrote anything with these photos and I'm glad because he didn't need to.

I want to see him so badly I feel it at the base of my throat, like heartburn but more romantic. Number Four on my list is hanging there, ripe to be checked off. Oh, what the hell. Since I'm riding a subway train in my fleece penguin pajamas and basically can't get any more pathetic today, I find his number in my phone and start typing.

Hi it's Kendall. Hope you had a good Christmas.
I'm back in town. Want to meet up?
SEND.

Of course, it might not actually send until I'm out of the subway, but the hard part's over.

"Kendall!" barks Emerson above the din of the train. "Did you hear me? We're getting off at the next stop!" He taps my elbow because he's learned this is an important step in getting and keeping my attention.

"Got it," I say. It wouldn't be the first time I missed a stop on public transportation. So much noise outside me, so much noise inside me, you'd think the roar would be deafening, but actually, it's the most soothing thing I've felt in days.

More suitcase trauma, and then we're on the street.

Holy crap, I'm back in a city again.

It's grown some magic since the last time I was here. Colors and brightness, sparkle and shine. It's amazing what electric lights and holiday window decorations will do to a generic street corner. Two blocks and two flights of steps later, we're at the apartment.

"Welcome," says Andrew as he opens the door and I follow them inside.

A fluffy black cat jumps down from something and rushes over.

"Louis!" says Em as he drops his bag and scoops up the cat. "Daddy and Papa are home!"

The apartment is small and cluttered, but in a way that seems carefully planned. "Nice," I say, looking around. "It's all really nice."

By *nice*, I mean, I want it. I want all of it.

"Want to see the guest room?" asks Andrew.

He leads me to a door, flashes me a big grin, and swings it open.

It's a closet.

With a bed stuffed inside. And clothes hanging from the rods.

"Um," I say.

"This is the whole reason we got this apartment," says Andrew proudly.

Emerson comes over and examines my face. "She does not look impressed."

"If she knew anything about the types of living space available to a pair of twenty-somethings like us, she would be," Andrew says.

"I *am* impressed," I say. "You've been talking about living together in Manhattan since five minutes after you met and now look, you're doing it. You're adults."

"Well, that remains to be seen," says Andrew, with a look over at Emerson, who's now burying his face in the cat's fur. "But we do like to pretend. And on that note, I have to change and get to the office."

I pull my suitcase into the closet. There's enough room for it to stand there at the end of the bed, but not to open it. Eh, I'll make it work.

After I've dug out some actual clothes and gotten dressed, I find Emerson sitting on the couch in the living room, the cat asleep on his lap. Andrew's gone.

"So," says Em as I sit down next to him. "Go ahead and check your phone again."

"Whatever do you mean?" I ask with a smile.

"You've been looking at your phone every sixty seconds. Who is he?"

"How do you know he's a he?"

Emerson laughs. "Sister, I've known you were straight since before I knew I was gay."

"His name is Jamie. I met him last summer. He's friends with Ari's boyfriend Camden."

"Oh, one of those Dashwood kids you told me about." Dashwood is the alternative private school Jamie attends. "Wait. He's not the guy who crushed your heart when he said he only liked you as a friend?"

"I wouldn't say *crushed*. Trampled a bit, maybe. It's much better now."

There's more to the story but I can't even think about it without wanting to puke, and since I don't want to puke on Emerson's cool beige couch, I'm not going to elaborate.

"So give me the details," says Emerson. "I need to live vicariously."

"When I was in Paris, I got an email from him out of the blue," I begin. "It was a photo of a man leaning out a window, with his head in his hands. The picture had this total 'I'm sorry' vibe. So I emailed him a photo back, one I took of a little girl holding a balloon in the Tuileries Garden. We've sent a bunch of pics back and forth since then."

Emerson raises his eyebrows. "Just photos?"

"Just photos. No text. No captions."

Emerson leans back and runs his hand along Louis's back. "That's pretty hot."

Yeah, it totally was. But now I want the words, and the sentences, and the paragraphs. I want everything.

Almost on cue, my phone dings.

DECEMBER 27

Max

I'M WAITING FOR MY FRIEND JAMIE AT THE G&S
Camera Store, wondering why someone would ever pay $2000
for a telephoto lens. Through the front window, I can watch the
parade of humanity going by. They say it's the most crowded
week of the year in New York City. Holy Reproduction, Batman.
There are a lot of people in the world.

When Jamie texted me last night that he was coming into
the city to meet up with some girl he's been e-flirting with, I
jumped at the chance for some company. I even invited him
to crash overnight at Big E's. My buddy is late but I don't even
mind because I'm out of the apartment. That's what spending
most of yesterday watching football with my grandfather has

done to me. We're talking English football here. As in, soccer. Big E likes to wax on about how this is a more nuanced sport.

If "nuanced" means nobody ever scores, then yes. Yes, it is.

"See that guy, the team owner?" Big E asked me at one point. "I went to college with him."

Of course this isn't true.

"Did you know him well?" I asked.

"Yeah, pretty well, for a while. Nice person, but he treated his girlfriend like garbage."

Then I asked, "How did you meet?" Big E ran with that for about twenty minutes of the most elaborate, detailed bullshit I've ever heard. In moments like that, I understand why he was such a legendary lawyer.

This is how I've seen my father and Aunt Suze interact with my grandfather. It's how I'm going to survive my days here. I'm going to ask him a lot of questions, and I'm going to answer all of his with a form of *yes*. Eventually, he'll get hungry or sleepy. (Preferably the latter.) There will be no talk about me, and why the hell I'm Not at College. No talk about a new home aide either, or plans to move him into a facility and sell his apartment for a gajillion dollars. There will be zero reason for him to throw the remote.

It must suck to outlive your wife, when everyone expected you to be the one to die first. To be given the gift of long life and not know what the hell to do with it. To be a sharp mind trapped inside a soft, weak, failing body.

Someone elbows me in the waist.

"Hey, man!" says Jamie when I turn around. He's got his backpack chest strap clasped shut and he looks so out-of-towner dorky, I cringe.

"Jamie!" I say, and we guy-hug. It's actually really, really good to see him. "You look different. It hasn't been *that* long, has it?"

"At least a month. Maybe more? Dude, why don't you ever drop by school for a visit?"

"Um, you know why," I say.

"Oh, yeah." Jamie's face falls. "I do."

The *why* has a name: Eliza.

"Well," I say, "I'm glad you'll be staying over so we can catch up." I look around the store. "So you're really going to buy that video camera you've been lusting after?"

Jamie grins and nods. "Christmas money just put me over the top."

A sales clerk nearby hears this and shifts into Perky gear. "Our video department is upstairs!" she says.

"There are departments here?" I ask. "There's an *upstairs* here?"

Jamie laughs at me. "Come on, I'll show you my world."

I give him shit for it, but really, I envy Jamie. He has a thing. A passion. A reason to keep his eyes open.

For me, that's always been a girl. Eliza, and then before her, Nadine, and before her, Iris. I could go on. It's only during the short breaks between these songs that I can really listen to myself. Up until now, though, I haven't heard anything remotely interesting.

In the video *department*, I accompany Jamie as he feels up every camera they've got on display. It's basically obscene, the way he gropes. Cups them into his hand and fondles the buttons. I feel like I should give him some privacy.

"Oh God," he moans. "This is the one I've had my eye on, and it feels even better in person than I thought it would."

Gross, right?

"When are you meeting up with this girl?" I ask, trying to bring us back to a PG rating.

"One o'clock," he says. "At the Met."

"Museum date. Nice."

"There's a photography exhibit we both want to see."

"Sounds cool. *She* sounds cool."

Jamie pauses for a moment and takes a breath like he's about to say something.

"So, how are we doing?" asks the salesclerk as she appears out of nowhere.

While Jamie buys the camera and arranges for it to be shipped to his house, I wander over to a wall of video monitors. I take a step and suddenly see myself on all of them. Not my whole self. My head and shoulders are cut off, but that's typical. When you're six foot three, you get used to parts of your body not fitting into things like camera frames. And portable toilets. And cars.

I examine what I do see. The body could be anyone's. If I didn't remember I was wearing a brown plaid scarf, I would have assumed it was a stranger's.

"Oh my God, that was exhilarating," says Jamie behind me. I turn to see him holding up a printed receipt for his purchase.

"Mazel tov," I say. "I hope you and your video camera will be very happy together."

We laugh. This feels good. It's been awkward with him since Eliza and I broke up, and our circle splintered.

"Come on," says Jamie. "I now have twelve dollars to my name and I want to spend it on hot dogs."

We step out onto the street. The sun's moved to a spot right between the buildings on either side of Seventh Avenue. It gives all the holiday lights a surreal middle-school-musical glow. We head uptown. At a sidewalk cart, Jamie buys us each two hot dogs, and I cover a pair of Cokes. We walk slowly and eat fast.

"So, Max. How's your life?" asks Jamie between bites.

"Aside from the fact that I'm living at home and my job makes me want to stick hot pokers in my eyeballs? It's stellar."

"Then, quit. Do something else."

"I'm making a lot of cash for school."

"There have to be other ways to do that."

Yes, there are. My mom's brother Jake invited me to come live with him in Seattle for a few months. He could get me an internship at his tech company. We could do some traveling. He laid it all out for me at Thanksgiving. I didn't tell anyone because I knew they'd all want me to go. Then they'd expect me to explain why I couldn't. How could I, when I can't even explain it to myself? It was easier to say *No, thanks.*

"It's only for a few more months," I finally say, then decide to change the subject. "How's Camden?"

"Happy," says Jamie. The simplicity of that causes me physical hurt.

Our buddy Camden fell in love with someone who's really good for him. I would never tell anyone this, but seeing Camden in a healthy relationship made me see just how unhealthy mine was.

In other words, really completely fucking unhealthy.

But when your girlfriend has been living in a toxic family environment for years, what do you do?

If you're me, you postpone your plans for college. You agree to stay in town, telling yourself it's mostly so you can work a humiliating job and earn money toward your first year's tuition. You give her everything she needs, emotionally and physically, plus the courage to seek help and call a youth hotline. You even walk her to her first Alateen meeting.

You watch her start to help herself and be okay.

Which is the moment you know you're done.

Which can be one moment too late to leave.

"I should get back and check on Big E," I say at the next corner. "Have fun with the girl. Text me when you're heading to the apartment, I'll come downstairs and meet you."

"Will do," says Jamie.

After another quick but significantly more awkward guy-hug, I walk away by myself. It's something I know I have to get used to.

Kendall

HERE COMES JAMIE, HOPPING TOWARD ME UP THE
front steps of the Metropolitan Museum of Art in a navy blue
down jacket and blue plaid scarf, his curly blond hair squirm-
ing out of a stocking cap. This is the guy who read my blog
and emailed me and sent me photographs every few days for
months. I heard from him more often than my best friend, Ari.
I was far away from everyone in my life and loving that feeling of being alone, but, you know. Alone is still alone. Jamie's
photos gave me someone extra special to carry around in my
pocket.

Needless to say, I'm overjoyed to see him. But I don't want
him to know that, so I just raise my hand and say, "Hey."

"Hi," he says back.

Then we hug. We're both wrapped in thick winter coats so it's not exactly titillating.

"How was your bus ride from New Paltz?" I ask.

"I had the best time peering down into the cars to spy on people. When did you get back?"

"A few days before Christmas."

He nods. Now here's the awkward silence.

"Should we get on line?" I ask.

Jamie breaks into a grin. "Lines? Lines are for suckers." He pulls some folded paper out of an inner coat pocket. "I already bought tickets through the website. My treat."

"You're smart," I say. "And sweet," I add, as if I'm someone who knows how to work the whole boy-girl system.

As Emerson had warned me, the museum is stupid-packed. But the crowd is comforting, because Jamie and I have to focus on navigating it, instead of on how to act with each other. We follow signs to the Henry Eisenkraft exhibit.

Eisenkraft is apparently a super-famous photographer and even though I'd never heard of him before yesterday, I was great at faking it. That's what Jamie and I first bonded over, photography, because at the time, that was my thing. Problem is, it's not anymore. I like taking photos, and I enjoy looking at photos (especially Jamie's), but I've moved on. Anyone reading my blog might have noticed that somewhere between London and Bath, I stopped posting ten pictures a day. This was around the time I got the idea for *Together at Midnight* and all my Thought Worms got excited about that.

I should mention here that this is a pattern for me. Not an excuse. Just some context.

In the first room of the exhibit, I can instantly see why Jamie is a fan. Eisenkraft's work is full of people and situations you wouldn't normally look twice at. A group of teenagers huddled against the brick wall of a factory, smoking cigarettes. Two kids and a cow in a field.

"This is what I love about the guy," says Jamie, stopping in front of a photograph of a woman holding a baby on a street corner, blurry cars going by. "He's all about these stolen moments, full of stories."

His whole face has lit up, examining the photograph.

"So tell me," I say. "What's the story here?"

Jamie stares some more and thinks. "She's waiting for someone to pick her up. A husband, maybe. She married him too young or just doesn't like the guy anymore. She's stuck with the kids. And all she can think of is that she'd rather get in any other car, any of the ones going by, than the one she has to."

"That's depressing."

"Then the image has done its job. You're affected. It changed you, even if it's only for a few seconds."

We move over to the next photo, a shot of two men in cowboy hats holding glass bottles at the back door of a restaurant. They both look like they want to cry and are terrified by that.

"Does his work get any happier?" I ask. "Is there maybe a room dedicated to his 'Prozac Years'?"

Jamie laughs. "Even if there were, nobody would want to see it."

After the exhibit, we spend the rest of the afternoon upstairs in the collection galleries. We wander separately but near each other, from piece to piece. Every so often, Jamie drifts close to me and whispers an observation or a joke, or sometimes mutters "I love this one" under his breath, like he's afraid to admit it to anyone in the world but me.

This is what I discovered in all those museums in Europe: when you really connect with a work of art, it doesn't matter that a million people have already stood where you're standing. The instant it means something to you, it's yours. I wonder if Jamie feels this way, too.

While we're sitting on a bench in a room full of Monets, a tour group seeps in. The guide starts explaining how and when these paintings came to the museum, and it takes me at least a minute before I realize she's speaking French. And I'm mostly understanding her.

I hear the artificial *click* of a cell phone photo and turn to see Jamie, snapping a picture of me.

"Why did you do that?"

"Stolen moment," he says with a shit-eating grin. "Full of stories."

Damn this boy.

We're walking through an atrium when Jamie checks his watch. Who wears a watch these days? He does.

"I have to go soon," he says. "I'm staying with a friend over-night, and I'm supposed to meet him for dinner."

Something deflates inside me. *Nooooo*, it sighs as the air rushes out. I don't want him to leave.

"Yeah, I should get back, too," I lie.

"How long are you staying in the city?"

"Not sure. A couple of days, maybe. I want to put off reality as long as possible."

He nods. "I hear you. Unfortunately, I have some reality I can't avoid, in the form of a ski trip with my folks." His eyes travel over my face, darting from feature to feature, and I can only wonder what he's looking for. "Will you be here for New Year's?" Jamie adds.

My throat tightens, but in a good way. New Year's. In New York City. That's a lot of pressure. That's like, diving into the ocean when you've just learned to swim.

"Yes," I say.

Jamie smiles. Maybe he found what he was searching for, in my face. "Let's meet back here on New Year's Eve."

"Right on this very spot?"

"Somewhere in the city, To Be Determined."

I almost say *It's a date!* But thank God, *thank God*, I catch myself. "That sounds perfect," I say instead.

"Where does your brother live?"

"Way uptown. Ninety-Sixth Street and First Avenue."

"My friend is on Park and"—he checks his phone— "Eighty-Second Street. Is that the same direction?"

"It totally is."

"Then let's walk." Jamie holds out his hand and for a second, I think I'm supposed to take it, but then I realize he's just indicating the way forward. Our next steps. I take that hand *mentally* and we cross Fifth Avenue. I lead him toward Madison.

"So, do you have your college apps in?" he asks.

Those two words together make me wince. I swallow hard and say the thing that could change everything about how Jamie sees me:

"Not yet. No rush for me. I'm just applying to the community college."

His eyebrows go way up but he doesn't look horrified.

"It's more my style right now," I continue. It's also more my speed, but when you bring up words like *speed* in connection to school, you also silently bring up words like *stupid* and *learning disabled* and for obvious reasons I don't want to do that here.

Jamie nods. "I hear they have a great art program."

"Yes!" For knowing that and saying that, I like him at least 5 percent more than I did. "The art department was actually a big draw for me. Until I get my grades up and figure out what else I might want to study, it'll keep me busy."

"Lots of kids from my school end up there," Jamie says, "before moving on to another college."

The Like-o-Meter jumps again.

"What about you?" I ask.

"I applied to seven schools, but my first choice is Wesleyan," he says. "Fingers crossed."

Wesleyan is somewhere in Connecticut, which means it's not too far away and we could have a doable long-distance relationship. Sure, I'll cross my fingers for Wesleyan.

"So tell me more about the trip," says Jamie after a few moments where we're walking in silence. "What was one amazing thing?"

I quiet my mind so something can slide in, and that's not easy for me, especially in a city. Even the dog peeing on the tree trunk up ahead makes noise in my brain. Finally, an image of a cathedral offers itself up.

"Visiting Canterbury, while we were reading *The Canterbury Tales*."

"Shit, that's cool. What else?"

The sun's beginning to set, and the lights on the buildings, in the trees, in the store windows take on a different, calmer glow that feels artificial and natural at the same time. We hang a left to head uptown and as we keep putting one foot in front of the other, I tell him more about the cities and places I visited. He listens like he cares.

Every step we take nudges the needle on my Like-o-Meter.

We hit the corner of Eighty-Second Street and Jamie stops dead, peers east toward Park Avenue.

"I guess I'm headed that way," he says.

"And I can get an uptown bus," I say, pointing to the bus stop at the curb.

We stand there for many seconds. It's so, so awkward. We're right outside a deli with bins of produce under an awning, and I stare the heck out of some grapefruit.

"I had a really good time today," says Jamie.

"Yeah, I'm glad we did this."

We're grabbing phrases out of a book (blue, small, but thick). *Things to Say at the End of a Date.*

God, I'm so tired of waiting for boys to kiss me. Of hoping, expecting, fantasizing.

You don't have to be her anymore, I remind myself, and I reach up to kiss him. First.

It's just a quickie. My lips skim his lips, like a pebble against the surface of water. They touch once before leaping away. Jamie's lips are cold and a little chapped. Surprised, but not horrified.

His eyes flicker and he smiles at me and reaches out. His fingers latch onto either side of my waist. Well, my waist buried deep inside my thick wool coat. Frankly, I'm surprised he can find it. He grabs the material and starts to pull me closer.

"Jamie?" someone asks.

I look up.

Oh. My. God.

Jamie looks up, too, then lurches away from me.

Standing behind us is a guy named Max.

I'm so shocked to see him, that he could actually be here, that I do the most inappropriate thing possible: I break out laughing.

Now Jamie's frowning at me and so is Max. Information begins arranging itself into neat rows in my head.

Max is the friend Jamie's staying with.

Jamie didn't mention that because he knows what Max and I did last summer.

Judging from the expression on Max's face—a cross between shock and anger, I'll call it *shanger*—he didn't know Jamie and I were hanging out.

I'm suddenly full of *shanger* myself, because Max is the last person I want to see right now. I can feel him staring at me, but I can't meet his eyes, physically can't turn my head even if I wanted to. He's Medusa and I'm whoever that other guy was. Theseus? Perseus? I get them mixed up, and anyway, why am I thinking about Greek myths right now? Because this is mortifying, that's why.

"Hey, man," asks Jamie in the most forced-casual voice I've ever heard. "What are you doing here?"

Max holds up a brown paper grocery bag. "Big E needed milk and roasted almonds."

This clearly makes sense to Jamie, because he nods. Then we're all silent again for a few moments.

"And I got us some Chinese takeout for dinner," adds Max, holding up a second bag in his other hand.

"Perfect," says Jamie, nodding again. Another pause is about to settle over us when he takes a deep, deep breath. "Fuck it," he continues. "I'm sorry, Max. I'm sorry I didn't tell you it was Kendall."

Max opens his mouth to say something, then changes his mind.

A bus approaches the stop. I have no idea which route it is, but it's headed uptown, away from this corner, and that's good enough for me.

"I should go," I say, throwing a quick thumb toward the bus.

"Wait!" says Jamie. "Catch the next one." His eyes are pleading and generally adorable. "This is not how I wanted the day to end. I should have told you I was staying with Max. I just didn't want this weird *thing* in the middle of our time together."

I huff a sigh, looking back at the bus. People have climbed on and the doors are closing.

"Okay," I say. We watch it pull away. Now what?

Jamie has not taken his eyes off me. Max is still standing there, a few feet from us, and I still haven't looked at him.

"Good," says Jamie. "Thanks. Will you . . . will you wait here a minute?"

"Why?"

"Just wait. I'll be right back."

Jamie steps back and holds his hands up like he's balanced me on something precarious. He pauses to see if I am, in fact, going to move. (I'm not.) Then he turns and runs past Max, into the deli.

Max exhales long and hard. "Hi," he says. "I didn't say that yet."

"Hi," I reply. I can do *hi.*

"How are you?"

"Good." I can do that, too. No problem.

"Are you heading back home tonight?" he asks. So we're going to trade small talk. This is tinier than that, really. It's microtalk.

"I'm actually crashing at my brother's place this week. I didn't know you were living here now."

"I'm not. Just staying with my grandfather for a few days."

I nod. We're silent again, and it's still horrible, but at least now I can look at the guy. He seems different than I remember him from the Night of the Nuclear Mistake. Still crazy tall, but his brown hair looks darker, and shaggier too. Parts of it are tucked behind his ears, but other parts have escaped. He still has what I consider one of the least boring noses I've ever seen, big and face-defining, with a bump in exactly the right place.

"Have you seen Ari and Camden lately?" Max finally asks.

"No. I've . . . I've been away."

"Oh, that's right! You went to Europe. Was it awesome?"

"It was awesome."

I really, really didn't want it to, but here comes the thinking anyway, about the minivan in the parking lot of that comic convention we all went to. *I was crying. Jamie had just told me he didn't think of me romantically. Max put his hand on my back, right between my shoulder blades.*

I wish I could remember who kissed who first. Or maybe it's better that I don't.

I glance at the bus stop, which has filled up with people again. It's one of the things I love about cities and public transportation: an endless tide of passengers, crashing and receding. Where is Jamie?

A young couple walks past us. "That was so embarrassing!" the girl barks at the guy.

"I had a right to be there!" the guy barks back.

"Well," says Max to me. "When you see them, tell them I said hi."

It takes me a second to realize he's still talking about Ari and Camden, and I'm about to respond when I'm distracted by the young couple again. The girl has stopped walking and now she's raising her voice.

"We're done! Do you understand? You cannot show up at parties you weren't invited to!"

"If you hadn't blown off my messages today," the guy says, air-jabbing his finger at her, "I wouldn't have had to do that!"

He's quite a few years older than us, late twenties maybe, wearing a sweatshirt and white pants, and the white pants seem out of place in the winter.

"Oh my God, you're such a dick and you don't even know it!" yells the girl. She's younger than the guy, wearing a long down coat and ballet flats. Her ankles must be really cold compared to the rest of her.

"And you're a dirty-mouth bitch!" shouts the guy.

There's no politely ignoring this, no it's-fine-this-happens-in-New-York-every-minute vibe. I can see a thought bubble hovering above every person on this corner. *Is this a situation? Should someone do something?* Just questions, though. No answers.

The girl mutters and starts to walk away from the guy, but he grabs her arm. "Get your hands off of me!" she spits. She scans the crowd at the bus stop.

I scan the crowd, too. There's a mother with a toddler in a stroller. An older couple with many shopping bags. A woman clutching a soft leather briefcase to her chest. And a middle-aged man with a guitar strung over his shoulder.

"Luna, you do this to me every single time," says the guy to the girl. "I'm not going to let it happen again."

I glance at the others. Is nobody going to ask the guy and girl if everything's okay?

The guy reaches out to grab the girl, but she makes a break for it.

Max

THE GUY CATCHES THE GIRL WITH A GENTLE GRAB AT her elbow.

"Go home," she says to him, her voice softer now. "This is over."

I wonder what's over. This conversation? Their relationship? There's something about her that reminds me so much of Eliza. I don't know this couple but my gut says they do this a lot. It's part of their dynamic. Regular steps in their dance. I've done a version of that dance myself.

Now the girl starts crying.

There's a handful of other people at the bus stop. A man

with a guitar is standing closest to the girl. He steps forward. He's about to do something. Offer the girl help, or tell the dude to back off. Good. He should. He's bigger than me and could defend himself, if things get real.

Except now the guitar man is stepping back. For some reason, my feet feel glued to my spot on the pavement.

The guy reaches one arm around the girl's middle and tugs her closer.

"Fuck you, no!" she yells, and struggles to pry his arm away.

I start forming words in my mouth: *Hey what's going on is everything okay here.*

But in the next instant, she's free of him. She's spinning into the street.

And in the next half instant, the horn of a bus. Then, the worst sound ever. Like a thud, crossed with a crunch, crossed with brakes screeching.

Now there's a scream, but it's coming from someone on the sidewalk.

"Oh my God," says another someone, whooshing past me.

It's Jamie. Carrying a bouquet of flowers that flap as he moves. He rushes into the street and kneels at the front of the stopped bus. Drops the flowers and they land at the girl's feet, which is all I can see of her.

I step backward, stumbling as I go. Holy shit. Shit, shit, shit.

Jamie isn't the only one at the girl's side. There are others, appearing from different directions as if they were all waiting in the wings of a stage. People are on their phones. Hopefully at least a few are dialing 911 and not simply taking a video.

This is when it occurs to me to look for the guy. The girl's guy.

He's gone.

But I do see Kendall, hovering behind the bus shelter, her face in her hands. I go over to her.

"No, no, no, no, no," she's whispering to herself.

"Kendall," is all I can say. My tongue feels huge and dry in my mouth. Now I realize I'm shaking.

"That didn't happen," she adds, and breaks down in tears.

Now there are sirens.

Look alive, Max. Don't be completely useless. "Come on," I say, pressing my hand lightly on Kendall's back. "In here."

I guide her into a sandwich shop, where others are gathered in the window to watch what's going on. I pull out a stool for her, and she sits.

"You should call someone," I say. Keeping my voice calm is helping the rest of me be calm. Or at least, faking it.

Kendall nods and takes out her phone. Tears still winding their way down her cheeks. She talks to someone named Emerson, her voice wobbly, catching on every other word. When she starts telling him what we saw, I move back over to the window. I'm not ready to hear this become a story so quickly.

The ambulance is pulling away. Jamie's standing on the corner, looking for us. I indicate to Kendall that I'm going back outside and she nods, continues talking.

"Tell me," I say to Jamie when I reach him. "Dead?"

Jamie's a pale guy, but right now he looks vampire-drained. "I don't know. They packed her up and whisked her away."

A police officer approaches me. "Did either of you boys see what happened?"

Jamie shakes his head and swallows hard. But I say, "Yes."

The cop takes out a pad of paper. "Go on."

So I do. I try to summarize what I saw and heard, without letting myself think about it. Just the facts, sir. By the time I'm done talking and the cop turns to another witness, I see Jamie putting Kendall into a cab. After it pulls away, he steps into the street to pick up the crumpled flowers. Stares blankly at them for a moment. Then tosses them in a trash can.

I look around. My bags of food have vanished. I don't even remember putting them down.

"Come on," I say, tugging Jamie away from the trash. *Be useful,* I say to myself. "Let's get out of here."

When we reach the awning of my grandfather's building, Jamie pauses and looks up at its Park Avenue facade. It has actual stone gargoyles at the top. He takes out his phone and snaps some photos.

I'm thinking, kind of a weird thing to do after watching someone get maybe-killed. Then again, a totally normal thing to do if you're in shock. Am I in shock, too?

"Hey, August," I say to the doorman. He's wearing a long

overcoat with tassels on the shoulders. The guy's worked here since I was a little kid.

"Mr. Levine," says August, pushing the elevator call button for us.

"Mr. Levine!" cackles Jamie, then doubles over laughing.

"We just had a really intense experience," I explain to August, clapping Jamie protectively on the shoulder. By focusing on Jamie, I don't have to deal with how freaked out I probably am.

"What's intense is this lobby," Jamie says. He's looking at the mosaic tile walls, the chandelier, the overstuffed leather couches I never see anyone, *anyone* sitting on.

"It's a different world, for sure," I say.

Jamie seems equally impressed with the elevator, which is only a standard elevator, but perhaps he doesn't get out much. He takes at least three pictures of its interior during the short ride to the third floor.

I hand Jamie our bags of replacement food, purchased from another deli two blocks out of the way. This lets me concentrate on sliding the apartment key into the lock as quietly as possible. I'm not sure why I feel the need to be so quiet. We can hear the TV on full volume through the wall.

Inside, Big E is out cold in his chair. Small mercies.

After we put my grandfather's groceries away, I lead Jamie down the hall to my aunt's room. I'm about to open the door when I find myself turning to Jamie, pointing to the other door. My father's old door.

"This is going to sound weird," I say, "but do you want to sleep in my room with me? There's already an air mattress. I think maybe you shouldn't be alone."

"Because I'm completely wigged out?" he asks, with a sad smile. "Yeah, an old-school slumber party is a good idea."

We put Jamie's backpack in my room, then settle into the den with sandwiches.

"Want to watch something?" I ask, grabbing the remote. This one looks pristine, living blissfully far from Big E's quick-tempered fingers.

"Sure," says Jamie as he slides onto the couch.

I flip through the channels, hoping one will offer what we need. A buddy cop movie, or anything with animals that talk. But my eyes glaze over and all I see on each channel is the bus stop, and different versions of what could have happened.

In one version, the guy with the guitar steps between the couple, as I'd expected him to do. *Click.* The woman with the stroller asks the girl if she needs anything. *Click.* The older couple yell at both of them to take their drama elsewhere. *Click.* Then there's me. Not standing frozen to the sidewalk.

I tell the guy to leave her alone, that she's made her wishes clear to him. Or I simply tell him to back off and give her space. He gets so upset, he runs away. *He's* the one who dashes into the street and gets mowed down. No, if we're going to reimagine this, let's cut out the tragedy and go all the way. The guy takes off, disappearing forever, and the girl realizes she deserves so much more. The next day, she meets someone who's perfect for her and they live happily ever after.

"You're thinking about her, aren't you?" asks Jamie.

"Her name was Luna," I reply. "Or at least, that's what the guy she was fighting with called her. You thinking about her, too?"

"Dude, her blood is on my sneaker."

I look at his sneaker. She is 300 percent more present in the room now.

"Maxie?" yells Big E.

"Coming!" I shout, jumping up and hurrying into the living room.

"I'm starving," he says.

I defrost a casserole and pour him milk from the deli. Jamie peeks his head out of the den.

"Who is that?" asks Big E when he sees him.

"My friend Jamie. Remember? I told you. He's staying the night."

I motion for Jamie to come join us. His face says *please don't make me* but he does it anyway.

"You look a lot like my son when he was your age," says Big E to Jamie. And you'd think that would be a compliment, but after he says it, my grandfather scrunches up his face. So, maybe not.

"Do you need a blanket, Big E?" I ask him.

He shrugs. I know he does. He's just pissed that someone has to put it on him.

After I've covered him up and refilled his sports water bottle and retrieved the remote from where it fell on the floor, Jamie and I go back down the hall.

"It's good you're here, man," he says.

This could mean so many things. I'd be happy if even one of them were true.

DECEMBER 28

Kendall

I'M BEING MOCKED BY A MAROON TUXEDO JACKET.

It's hanging above my feet in the guest room/closet, all sharp-cornered and neat and simple. Me, I'm none of those things, especially right now.

I can tell it's morning, not because of the light because there is no light, but because of the sound of the coffeemaker and hushed, worried voices coming from the living room.

After Emerson met me at the cab and brought me upstairs last night, we lay on his bed together, flat on our backs with our heads touching.

"Do you want to talk about it?" he'd asked me.

"No, thanks."

Talking about it meant telling him the whole story, about the standing and the watching. That girl and guy must have been fighting for a good three minutes. I heard him call her Luna, I think. Three minutes of him bullying her, three minutes of me doing nothing. Well, not just me. Max, too. And one, two, three, four, five other people (I'm not counting the kid in the stroller). But Emerson thinks I just saw a girl step into the street and get hit by a bus.

"You could have PTSD," Emerson had said. "I'm a teacher. I'm trained to deal with this stuff."

"Please don't sound so excited about it," I told him.

Now I haul myself out of bed, purposely messing with the tuxedo jacket while opening the door. One shoulder sags halfway off the hanger, and I already feel better.

"Monkey's up!" chirps Andrew when I emerge from the closet.

"Did you sleep?" asks Emerson, furrowing his brow. Oh my God, it's the same brow furrow as Mom's. There is just no escaping it.

"More or less," I say, and even that's a lie. Emerson doesn't understand that I don't really sleep because the Thought Worms are against it, and they are especially rebellious after a day and evening like that.

Andrew says, "I was just telling your brother that I can work some press contacts to find out what happened to her."

Her. I almost like that better than an actual name, like she's a proper noun that doesn't need explaining.

"Can you do that?" I ask.

"He can try," says Emerson. "It might be on the news, too. If there was security footage."

A wave of horror hits me. I can see it now: a viral video of the "incident" and those of us standing by, doing nothing. *Another example of New Yorkers not giving a damn! Modern apathy!*

"I'd rather wait and see what Andrew can dig up," I say, and sink into the chair.

Andrew pours me a cup of coffee. "There's bagels," he says.

I nod, but honestly, I'm not sure I'll ever be hungry again. My phone, which I left on the kitchen counter, vibrates to let me know I have a message waiting.

Holy shit, says the text from Jamie. **I still can't believe that happened. Feeling freaked out. Headed back upstate now. Let me know how you're doing.**

I text him back **Doing okay, talk soon** and then think about this boy, although it feels like I'm not allowed to. Me kissing him and our breath mingling together in those moments before Max showed up. Before everything showed up.

Now I'm picturing Luna again, because she must have had a first kiss with that guy. There must have been a time when she was thrilled at the thought of him touching her, at all the possibilities that sparked.

Luna. I will let myself think about her more. She's dead or in a coma, or awake, but suffering. How can we not know what happened next? Stories have endings, dammit. They shouldn't trail off into multiple choice.

"I have to get to work," says Andrew, shrugging into his coat. "I'll call later if I snag some info for you."

Emerson and I both watch him tug his gloves on, finger by finger. These precise movements confirm for me that he's the owner of the taunting tuxedo jacket.

Andrew kisses us both good-bye and when he's gone, Em turns to me.

"When's Mom getting here?"

Oh, crap. I totally forgot about Mom, and about *Wicked* and her being upset and basically everything else in my life. I check my phone and there's a message waiting from her, too.

"She says she's coming in at three so we can have an early dinner first."

I can't talk to my mother about what happened and I can't explain why.

"Want to come with me to return all the ugly stuff I got for Christmas?" asks my brother.

I can't talk to him either, because he wasn't there and I already omitted vital information from the story. I really want to call Jamie, but I'm afraid talking about Luna will kill off everything good about yesterday. I still want the everything good. Is that selfish and shallow of me?

Suddenly, I know what comes next.

"There's something I have to do," I say, "but can I meet up with you later?"

*　*　*

I walk west from the apartment. It's cold but sunny, and all that's left of the snow that fell before Christmas is a few blackened piles of slush in random corners.

I cringe at the sight of every bus and stand a good five feet from each curb when waiting for the lights to change. Every time I hear a raised voice behind me, I freeze and turn to see who it came from. The city goes about its business, even though something bad happened. Then again, bad things happen all the time, everywhere.

It does feel better to be out on the street, part of normal life, although of course this is not *my* normal life. I'm just borrowing it, really, until I can find one of my own.

The intersection of Park Avenue and Eighty-Second Street is over fifteen blocks away but I get there more quickly than I expected. There are apartment buildings on all four corners and I have no idea which is the one I want.

"Hi," I say to the doorman at the first building. "Is there a guy named Max staying here?"

It sounds even weirder coming out of my mouth than I thought it would. The doorman gives me a confused, slightly wary look, like I'm one of those situations they've trained for.

"I mean, I'm looking for a friend. He's staying with his grandfather, but I don't know his grandfather's name."

The doorman shakes his head firmly and with certainty. "I'd know if there was someone staying with a grandfather. Sorry."

"Okay. Wrong building, I guess. Thanks."

A similar exchange happens at the next building, and I really, really want to take it as a sign to just abandon this idea.

"You must mean Mr. Levine!" says the doorman at the third building.

"That's Max?" I ask. "Or his grandfather?"

"Both. Is he expecting you?"

"No," I say, and I'm about to explain when the doorman makes a call. I turn to the gigantic lobby mirror and glare at my reflection.

"He'll be right down," says the doorman as he hangs up.

I sit on a leather couch. The lobby reminds me of a room in a French chateau our Movable School group visited in the Loire Valley.

The elevator dings.

"Kendall?"

I turn and there's Max, looking confused and surprised but maybe not in a bad way.

"Hi."

"Jamie left about a half hour ago to catch the bus."

"I know." We're silent again. If I can't even talk about this to Max, with whom I have nothing to lose, why am I here?

Max comes over to the couch and when he sees me sprawled on it, he smiles a bit, a smile edged in sadness. There's something protective about the way he stoops over me, although he probably stoops for everyone.

"What?" I ask, sitting up straight.

"Did you have as bad a night as I did?" he asks.

I let out a sigh that sounds a lot like a sob. "If your night was hellish, then yeah."

Max laughs and looks relieved. "I'm so glad somebody else knows what this feels like."

There's no need to explain what *this* means and it can't really be named anyway.

"You want to get some breakfast?" asks Max.

Don't cry, you dork. Don't you dare cry.

I nod, biting my lip so hard that it bleeds.

We're walking toward Lexington Avenue and the silence pushes against me from the inside. I really suck at silence, even in mortifyingly awkward situations like this. *Especially* in mortifyingly awkward situations like this.

When I can't take the pressure of it anymore, I ask, "So you're just hanging out with your grandfather until the semester starts?"

"Well, yes and no," Max says. "There is no semester. I deferred school for a year."

"Oh. I didn't know that."

More silence. Dammit, he's going to make me ask. Maybe I can control myself.

"Then what have you been up to since you graduated?" Okay, so, maybe not.

"Not much at all," he says. I sense the baggage in that statement. He's saying a lot even though it doesn't sound that way.

"How's Eliza?" I ask, because we already know I can't control myself.

After a few seconds, Max replies, "I hear she's okay. It's been a while since we talked."

I pause, nearly tripping over my own feet, then fall into step again.

"You guys broke up?"

"At Halloween."

"I'm sorry to hear that," I say. And I am, really. Because I probably had something to do with it.

"Her favorite holiday. Not the best timing, but that's how it went down." I glance at him and he's glancing back at me. There's a moment of *oh crap* and then we both look away. "It's all good now, we're friends," he adds.

Then he stops and points to a coffee shop, an old-school one, all vinyl and fluorescent lights like on the *Seinfeld* reruns I watch with my dad. Max opens the door for me and we rush inside to grab a window booth.

"Jamie said that before everything happened, you guys had a good time together," Max says as he unwraps his plaid scarf and tucks it next to him on the seat.

"Are those the words he used? *A good time?*"

Max thinks. "It might have been *amazing* or *awesome*. One of the really good *A* words."

"Okay, I'll take that," I say. I picture the flowers Jamie bought for me. I try really hard to picture him buying them, handing a deli clerk his money with a giddy smile. Not in Jamie's hand as he ran toward the girl, and definitely not lying in the street.

Maybe if I had done something to help Luna, or even helped someone help her, this morning would be different. I'd be sitting across from Jamie right now.

A waitress comes over. "Coffee," says Max. I nod at him. "Make that two." When she leaves, he leans toward me, his eyes so wide and round. I forgot that he has these baby-calf eyes; they're hard to avoid looking at. "It's disgusting coffee, but I like the vibe. My grandmother's been taking me here since I was a kid. I mean, she did. She died last spring."

I'm about to say the expected "I'm sorry" when the waitress comes back with a pitcher of coffee, pours us each a cup. I put my hands on it and even though it's only lukewarm, it still feels good.

"Her name was Luna," I blurt out.

"You heard that too?" We don't need any context here, which is cool and heartbreaking. "I thought that's what he said. I wasn't sure, but you were closer than I was."

"What's that supposed to mean?"

Max's eyes go even wider, if that's possible, and he shakes his head. "Nothing! Only that you could hear better. Not that . . . you should have . . ."

"Right," I say. "Sorry."

I've just given away how guilty I feel. But this is surprising: I don't mind. It's a relief, actually. Max opens his mouth like he wants to say something, then stops himself. I take a sip of my coffee, and he's right, it's total crap. Definitely not good enough to fill another awkward silence, so I do it myself.

"My brother's boyfriend is trying to find out what happened to her. You know, where they took her. How she is. *If she is, you know.*"

Max puts down his coffee cup and slides his hands toward me on the table. Not exactly reaching out, but wanting to. His hands are giant, the fingernails bitten down to stubs. I get a flash of those hands on either side of my face as we kissed last summer. *Block that out. Block block block.*

"Will you let me know if you hear anything?" he asks, then swallows hard. "I'll give you my number."

He fishes a pen out of his coat pocket and writes on a corner of the paper place mat, tears it off and hands it to me. I nod and stuff it into my purse.

Silence again, and it's excruciating. Knives in your ears or a hand on your throat would be nothing compared to this, I'm sure.

But the crazy thing is, I don't want to leave.

Max

DID I REALLY JUST GIVE KENDALL MY NUMBER?

I guess when something like Luna happens, rules of engagement go out the window. Yeah, from now on, this is how I'm going to refer to last night. Better than "That Thing" or simply "It." Which would be dumb. And cowardly. Saying her name, even if it's only in my head, gives her a tiny fraction of what I didn't give her on the street corner.

Also, if Kendall's going to date Jamie, we're going to have to figure out a way to deal with each other. Maybe, eventually, we'll talk about what happened in the minivan. Maybe we'll be friends.

"Maybe we can be friends," I blurt out.

Kendall wrinkles her nose, distorting the pattern of freckles on it. Then, she laughs. "We should totally be friends."

"Can we start right now?" I ask. Like I said: rules of engagement, totally gone.

She laughs again, smiling, and starts twirling a strand of her auburn hair around one finger. I take that as a yes. All this time, I've been trying really hard not to look at her lips. Because I've kissed them. I'd had too much to drink and it was an epically weird day, but if I told you I didn't remember what they tasted like, I'd be lying. I do remember. Everything about those minutes with her, I remember.

Maybe someday, I'll be able to think about it without the image of Eliza's face staring at me through the car window. Will there ever be a time when I don't think about Eliza's face? The angry one? Or any of her faces? (She had a lot.)

The waitress comes back and we both order the Two-Egg Special. Kendall adds a third creamer to her coffee. I've been counting. My grandmother always took four. I'm really curious to see if Kendall will match that.

"I keep running through those last few seconds in my head," I say.

She nods. Then tears well up in her eyes. (Green eyes, bright, even in a dark minivan in a hotel parking lot.) She closes them and says, simply, "Me, too."

"I could have done something. *Should* have done something."

Kendall nods again, eyes still closed. "Ditto."

"I was searching around online last night," I add. "There's

something called Bystander Syndrome. The more people watching something bad happen, the less likely any one person is to act."

Her eyes pop open. "That's fucked up."

"They've done studies. Each person thinks someone else is going to step in. I thought the guy with the guitar was on top of it."

Her face drops. She takes a sip of her coffee, then puts it down. Reaches for that fourth creamer as she says, "And I thought that older lady was going to give them both a piece of her mind. . . . It feels a little better, knowing there's a name for what we did. Or didn't do."

I think about that. I'm not sure it makes me feel better, but it does make me feel human.

I stare out the window. The movement of the cars and people on the street syncs up with music playing on speakers in the coffee shop. I could live in New York City if it were always like this. Like one eternal movie montage.

"I'd give anything for a redo," says Kendall, and takes a sip of her coffee. The waitress arrives with our breakfast. It smells like everything you ever dreamed about breakfast. I realize I'm ravenous.

"A redo would be awesome," I say, thinking about not just Luna, not just the minivan, but the last four months.

"Maybe we can make one," suggests Kendall, fresh energy in her voice. "Do what we should have done last night, but for someone else."

"That was a pretty unique situation. You want to go on patrol, looking for couples fighting?"

"I guess you're right," she says, then turns to stare out the window. "I guess I'm looking for a way to feel less guilty. Watch me give money to every homeless person I see today."

My grandmother used to do that. A crisp five-dollar bill to anyone who'd ask, and many who didn't. But only when Big E wasn't with us. He disapproved of handouts. If he was there, and they'd pass someone panhandling on the street, they'd walk on by without a second glance.

"Giving change to strangers isn't really the same thing as stopping a person from getting hit by a bus," I say, then realize I sound like a jerk.

"I know," says Kendall. She visibly deflates. "I guess I want to help someone. Be kind. Nobody does enough of that."

"Speak for yourself. I help people all the time." She raises an eyebrow at me, so I continue. "My grandfather, for instance. I'm sort of taking care of him, until we can hire a new home aide." *And I put off college for Eliza*, I want to add. Also: *I was helping you that night in the van, listening to you weep about Jamie.*

"That's great," says Kendall, "but that's different from reaching out to a stranger. Doing something unexpected, in the moment."

"Random acts of kindness."

"It's corny, I know." She shrugs.

I repeat it to myself. *Random acts of kindness.* "What are we talking here? Buying someone a coffee or paying their subway fare?"

Kendall thinks about that, then shakes her head. "Money's the easy way. It's not real kindness."

"Real kindness is easy, too."

"You think?"

"You just have to do it."

"You make it sound so simple," she says with a laugh.

"It is."

Now Kendall shakes her head. "I disagree."

"So do I," says a voice. We both glance up. The waitress has been clearing the table next to us. Eavesdropping. She steps over to us, her arms filled with dirty dishes. "Kindness is surprisingly hard. Take it from someone who serves a hundred strangers a day."

"See?" says Kendall.

I look at the waitress again. Her name tag says ERICA. She's in her forties, with very short, almost spiky, dark hair. Her glasses have black frames with white polka dots on them. Her round dangly earrings are made to look like green Christmas tree ornaments.

"I'd love to prove you wrong," I say. Hoping that sounds respectful, but dismissive.

"I'd love that, too," says Erica. There's a sudden glint in her eye. She puts the dishes down on our table, rests her hands on her hips. Confident, but calm about it. "Know what? Kids are into dares, right?"

Kendall and I exchange a look. Are we?

"Sure," says Kendall.

"Okay, I'm going to give you a dare. I dare you to perform random acts of kindness toward strangers today and let me know how that goes."

"No problem," I say. "How many do you want?"

Erica shrugs, but Kendall reaches into her bag and pulls out a little notebook. Her doodles are actually really good. Intricate. Lovely. She grabs the pen I left on the table and starts writing.

Mom with stroller.

Older couple.

Woman with briefcase.

Guy with guitar.

Max.

Me.

I see all those frozen faces again. I feel my own. That air of anticipation, each of us wondering who was going to step in. Who was going to be the one.

Kendall pushes the paper toward me. "There were seven of us standing there." Now she looks at Erica.

"Okay, then," says Erica. "I dare you to do seven acts of kindness." The spark in her eyes is really blazing now.

"In one day?" asks Kendall.

Erica thinks for a moment. "How about, by the end of the year? Midnight on New Year's Eve. That gives you four days."

"No money involved?" Kendall seems to actually be taking this seriously.

"No money."

"Not a problem. I have none anyway."

"What do we get if we're able to do it?" I ask Erica.

She considers the question, then breaks into a grin. "You kids come back here on January first with proof, and our cook will make you our best off-the-menu breakfast. I can also make sure you get on the wall." She points with her chin to the wall of framed photos. Regulars and celebrities from over the years. My grandmother wanted so badly to be on that wall. When the owner heard about her cancer, she finally made it. I imagine my photo next to hers, forever in this place we loved together. For a reason she'd be really proud of.

"Okay," I hear myself saying. "It's on."

Kendall takes a sip of her coffee, then slams the cup down. She's being dramatic. Funny. "I'm in, too."

"Smackdown," I add.

"Rumble in the jungle."

Erica laughs. "You kids just made my day, and it's still the breakfast shift."

"So how do we handle the, you know, scorekeeping?" asks Kendall.

"You tell me," says Erica.

"I guess there will have to be an honor system involved. But how about we get some kind of evidence each time," Kendall offers. "Like, a photo. Tangible stuff we can text each other with."

"Figure it out," Erica says as she pulls a check from her apron pocket, slaps it on the table. Then she gathers the dishes back up and walks away.

"Did we actually agree to something?" asks Kendall.

I shrug. "We'll never see her again, so not really. Not if we didn't want to."

"You were just being polite?"

"Yeah," I say. "I think she was only teasing us." I grab the check and pull it toward me. "Let me get this."

"Thanks," Kendall says.

Painful silence again.

"I should probably go," she adds, and starts wriggling out of her side of the booth. "I'm supposed to meet up with my brother. . . . Thank you for breakfast. It helped. Not the food, I mean, but . . ."

"I know what you mean."

Kendall nods, and I see her swallow hard. Then she puts on her coat, bright red wool with those black peg buttons. It should clash with her auburn hair, but somehow it doesn't. She pulls on her knitted hat and takes a long time wrapping her scarf around her neck—I count three full loops—and pulls on mismatched gloves. One looks much too big, like it's a guy's.

"Catch you later," she says, and leaves the coffee shop. Through the window, I watch her cross in the middle of the street and get lost in the crowd on the other side.

She barely touched her food.

I slide the plate toward me and grab my fork.

Luna

THERE'S A LOT OF LIGHT.

Not bright exactly. Just, a fucking lot of it. It's everywhere.
Like behind my eyeballs.

Luna, the light says. Maybe it's not the light saying that.
Because that would be stupid, light saying my name. And anyway, it sounds like a dude. I've never thought about it until this
second, but I know light would not have a dude voice.

The dude says my name like I'm in trouble. Which I definitely am.

I know that, too.

Trouble.

Wrong.

Yeah, no question about that.

Because I can't move my head or my arms.

"Luna," the dude says again. The next time, my name goes high at the end like a question. "Luna?"

Urrrrr, I say. It's the first thing that comes to mind. Also, the only sound I can make.

"Luna, can you hear me? My name is Dr. Effron. You're in the hospital."

Urrrrrmmmm. That's an improvement.

"You were in an accident. Can you open your eyes for me?"

Can I open my eyes? WTF, they're already open. They're open and I'm in a white room where a thousand colors flash against the walls. It's sort of cool.

But then I remember. Rooms have doors, right? There's a tugging feeling somewhere at the base of me. I should open the door. It's suddenly super-important that I open the door. This doctor is waiting on the other side and he really, really wants to see me.

I feel around for a doorknob. There's got to be one somewhere. I run my hand against the flat cold of the wall, then the next, then the next, and the next. Four walls make a room. Why the fuck is there no knob?

So I just push. Suddenly, the wall gives way, like I found the exact spot where there's a hole in it. The hole expands as I push my hand farther through.

Now I'm ripping the wall.

Now there really is light everywhere. Way, way, way too much light. And pain.

So. Much. Pain. This was a bad idea.

"Luna," says the doctor again. He looks happy.

Okay, so I'm here.

Give me a reason to stay.

Kendall

THE WIND WHIPS DOWN LEXINGTON AVENUE, MAKING
the traffic light cables jiggle. I pull down my hat and yank my
scarf up over my nose and think about the bad, hot coffee in
the cozy, warm booth across from Max. I wish I could have
stayed longer and that wishing takes me by surprise, because
it was a wacko situation, sitting there with him. But now out
here on my own again, I miss it. Can something be difficult
and comforting at the same time?

I take the subway to meet Emerson in the housewares
department at Macy's. (No buses for me, for a while, or ever
again.)

When I find my brother, he's holding a French press that

Sullivan gave him and Andrew for Christmas. He's returning it because, duh, they already have two.

"Hey, do you practice Random Acts of Kindness?" I ask instead of saying hello.

"I'm a teacher," he says with a little snort. "Of course I practice Random Acts of Kindness. For instance, not smacking a student when he or she really needs to be smacked."

Emerson freezes, then looks furtively around us.

"I guess I shouldn't make these kinds of jokes in public."

"I'm being serious," I say. "What do you think of the whole idea? Someone just dared me to commit random acts of kindness to strangers, saying it's harder than it sounds."

"Have to say, I agree with that," says Emerson. "The term looks great on a bumper sticker, but what does it really mean? Kindness isn't objective, you know. One person's kindness is another person's . . ."

Emerson pauses. His eyes catch a fancy ceramic casserole dish. He reaches out to run his finger along the ridges, which must not feel quite right because he abruptly pulls his finger away and walks on.

"Intrusion," he finally continues.

"But isn't that the kind of thinking that results in people standing by, letting bad things happen?" I ask.

"Maybe. But how can you even tell when someone needs your kindness? If you don't know someone personally, it's really hard to identify these things."

He's right, of course. I look around the crowded store.

Everyone seems pretty frazzled.

"We're all so used to keeping our shit together," continues my brother. "We don't show our weaknesses."

"That's true."

"Be kind, for everyone you meet is fighting a hard battle."

I grab Emerson's arm and he turns to look at me.

"What?" I ask.

"It's a poster in our school counselor's office," says Emerson with a shrug. His face softens. "I quote it to the kids a lot, when they need to show some compassion."

I get this instant, overwhelming feeling that Emerson is a great teacher and that his students love him a lot.

"I have to remind myself of that all the time," he adds. "All. The. Time."

He moves off, leaving me to ponder the saying. *Everyone you meet is fighting a hard battle.* Yes, I can believe it. I sit on one of the miniature made-up beds that I used to think were for the elves who lived in department stores and only came out at night.

A few minutes later, Emerson appears with a huge pillow and motions for me to follow him to the register.

"You're exchanging a coffee press for a pillow?" I ask him.

"It's a really, really nice one."

"Way to live on the edge, Em." Although this seems so adult to me; you know you're finally grown-up when you have to purchase your own bedding.

The line's long. A second after we take our spot, a guy steps in behind us, a baby in a carrier strapped to his chest. He's holding a little girl by one hand and in the other, a shopping bag overstuffed with a down comforter.

The guy sighs, like he's annoyed we got there first, and I'm annoyed that he's annoyed.

"Ow," yells the girl. "You're holding too tight!" She squirms out of his grip and shakes her hand.

"Okay," says the guy. "If you can be a big girl and stay with Daddy, you don't have to hold my hand."

The girl nods, and we all stand there for ten seconds in silence.

Then the kid turns and walks away.

"Goddammit, Sophie!" the dad yells.

Sophie slowly turns around and circles back to the line, then sticks her finger in her ear and starts digging for gold. Seconds later, she's drifting again. It's like I'm watching my own self from ten years ago.

"You are going to be in so much trouble when I tell Mommy," says the dad. The girl stamps one foot and marches back to the line.

Emerson gives me a look. "Andrew wants kids someday," he whispers. "I'd rather get a dog."

I glance at the dad and am mortified to see he's staring at us. Clearly, he's heard what Emerson said, but instead of being offended he just seems terribly sad.

"Good call," he says to Emerson. We all laugh, including the baby.

The guy's dad-radar must go off, because he snaps his head around and sure enough, his daughter is gone again.

"I'm going to kill her!" he mutters, then looks at us, embarrassed. "Not really. Be right back . . ."

When the dad returns a minute later with his daughter, she's crying. "But I'm SO BORED!"

"Sorry, sweetie. As soon as we're done here, we'll get you a treat. I promise."

The line moves forward and Emerson hangs back, motioning for them to go in front of us.

"Thank you," says the dad.

I grab Emerson's arm. "Hey! That was an RAK!"

It takes Emerson a second to figure out that stands for Random Act of Kindness. He laughs. "You're right."

"That wasn't hard at all."

"Would you have thought of it?" he asks.

"Yes!" I say. "I think. Pretty much."

Now we're waiting again, and the little girl looks at me with these big, pleading eyes. Oh my God, I totally know how she feels because being the baby sister of three much older brothers, I was toted around a lot. I waited, *a lot*. When Mom took us all shopping, I'd climb inside the racks of boys' clothing, feeling the stiff denim-like walls on either side of me. I made forts out of the folding seats of basketball gyms and collected flowers in the outfield of every baseball diamond in the county.

Suddenly, I'm doing something without thinking: I'm pulling my phone from my coat pocket and turning on the camera.

"Here," I say to the girl. "Why don't you take some pictures of us? I'm Kendall, and this is my brother Emerson."

Sophie takes the phone and points to the baby. "That's my brother Aidan. But he's asleep and boring."

I catch her father's eye. "Is that okay?" I ask him, indicating the phone, and he nods.

I put my arm around Emerson and make a goofy face while Emerson does bunny ears over my head. Sophie thinks this is the funniest thing she's ever seen and takes about twenty-seven pictures.

"Okay, now we need to do one like this," I say, and grab Emerson in a headlock.

More little-girl cackles as other people in the line turn around to watch. Sophie points the cell phone at her dad and snaps a picture of him smiling at her.

"Take another," he says. "I wasn't ready."

He takes off the baby's little wool cap and sticks it on top of his own head. This officially sends Sophie into hysteria.

A customer service clerk waves over Sophie's dad. When he steps up to the counter, Sophie doesn't go with him and instead lingers with me. I show her an app on my phone that lets her distort the photos she just took. While her dad's busy returning the mammoth comforter, she makes my features swirl around like water in a toilet bowl.

Finally, the guy steps away from the counter and toward us.

"Thank you again," he says.

"No problem," I say. It really wasn't.

"Come on, kiddo." He grabs Sophie's hand and tugs her away. He's holding so tight, I can see how much it probably hurts.

When I look at my phone, it's covered in dirty, sticky finger-prints, but I can't help but smile.

I find Max's number in my purse and start typing a message to him.

Guess what? I'm going to do Erica's dare. Already one down.

A few seconds later, he replies. **For real?**

Was it for real? So I kept a kid entertained for a few minutes when she needed it most. Still, I could have stood there and continued to let her irritate the hell out of everyone. I'm going to count it.

I have photographic proof and an eyewitness, I type to Max.

I'm about to ask him to join me when another message comes in. This one's from Andrew.

Ken, I got some information on that girl. Call me.

Brian Cheng

I'M A GOOD HUSBAND AND THAT'S WHY I'VE VOLUN- teered to take the kids out for the day. Stephanie needs to sleep. She needs to sleep in our bed with the comforter that's been peed on a hundred times by cats as well as humans. I bought her another but it was the wrong size because I'm an idiot who doesn't know the difference between a queen and a California king. She needs to sleep because she ran herself ragged making a perfect Christmas for the kids and I'm the one who got her a gift that has to be returned. Good job, douche bag.

I need to sleep, too. What I wouldn't give for a day of binge-watching *Breaking Bad* in my underwear. Sometimes, I wish

I was seriously ill so I could get checked into a hospital for a little while.

My problems aren't unique. There are five billion families in New York City and we're all just trying to make it work. "Move up to the suburbs," some people say. "It's better up here!" But Stephanie won't. She can't. She grew up in Manhattan and believes her kids should, too.

Right now, fatherhood is basically this: the baby sleeps and cries and this carrier kills my back. Sophie adores me until she hates me and says, "Screw you, Daddy!" which is apparently something she learned from the doorman.

And I am so tired. All the time. The kind of tired where you feel like you're being tugged down into the earth's core.

Still. I look for moments of joy. When I see my children laughing. When I see something through their eyes, something I've seen a thousand times before and thought was stupid but now it's awesome. I think kids exist mostly to remind us that not everything is stupid. That there's still discovery in the world.

But even with those moments, most of the time I'm looking for the village that's supposed to be out there, willing to help me raise my family. I haven't found it. Or maybe I have, but the villagers are chasing me down with torches. Because I've done nothing right. Every call has been a bad one and my kids are terrible, irreversible brats.

Every once in a while, someone puts down the torch and

holds out their hand. Like that brother and sister on line at Macy's.

That's the world I want my kids to inherit.

At which point, I'm getting into bed and watching *Breaking Bad* for about five weeks straight.

Max

ELIZA IS SCREAMING MY NAME. I CAN'T SEE HER. I can only hear her.

She's scared. She's in pain. Truly in pain, and not just pretending. I've learned the difference.

I can't tell if someone's hurting her. I can't tell where she is, exactly. I'm on the playground at school and first, I hear her in front of me. Then, behind me. Then from somewhere above.

Just to make things interesting and maybe a little cliché, a huge snake loops itself around one of my ankles. It begins to squeeze tight.

I wake up covered in sweat. The radiator by the window hissing. Late afternoon sun pours through the window, filtered by the glass into a million visible dust particles. And I am, in fact, hearing my name being called. Not by Eliza, but my grandfather.

I didn't mean to fall asleep. When I came back to the apartment after coffee with Kendall, Big E was out cold. I lay down in my dad's bedroom to read. Must have crashed when the coffee wore off.

"Max!"

I sit up and shake the remaining fragments of the dream out of my head. Even though I couldn't see her in the dream, Eliza's face lingers. Her long black hair, so straight it always reminded me of a curtain. There were always streaks of blue where the light hit it the right way. Her dark eyes that always seemed to be pleading for something. When she was acting like she didn't need anything, those eyes gave her away. I noticed it. Every time.

In my mind, I see Eliza's pale skin. Then I feel it. Soft and always a little cold. Her fingertips on my arm. Her mouth on my neck. All the blood in my body rushing toward her.

And now I have a boner. Fantastic.

No, I tell the Eliza-in-my-head. You don't have this kind of power over me anymore.

I'm just horny and lonely and lost. Anything would do it. *Anyone.*

I get out of bed and pull on an extra sweatshirt. The last thing I need is Big E noticing my pants-tent. Although he would probably enjoy it. Tell me some stories I would be fascinated and horrified to hear.

"Maxie!"

"Just a sec!"

I find Big E standing in the kitchen. As in *on his feet* and *upright*.

"Big E!" I exclaim, and rush to his side. There's really no reason for that. He's bracing himself against the counter.

"I was going to pour myself some coffee, but there's none made."

"I fell asleep. Sorry. Had kind of a rough night."

I pull out one of the stools and he lowers himself onto it. For a moment, I wonder if the thing might break. It's been around. Big E has always been tall. Like my dad, and like me. But now he's wide, too. Which he has totally earned. I can't wait to be allowed to get fat.

"You and your friend up late?" he asks.

"Yeah. Something happened on the street that shook us pretty hard."

As soon as I say them, I wish I could inhale the words back in. Big E is not the guy you pour your soul out to. He won't have any words of wisdom. Not even something that sounds cryptic at first, but makes sense later. Only TV and movie grandpas do that.

I start making his coffee. Despite everything I know about the universe, I find myself hoping he'll ask me to elaborate. *Tell me what happened, Maxie.* This guy has lived in Manhattan most of his life. He's seen some stuff, for sure. He might have some perspective stored away.

Instead, he says, "I should have given you boys money to go to Shea O'Malley's, so you could have a few for me."

I start to say the obvious. We're underage. I don't like bars. But that's against the policy of Yes that I've been asked to stick to.

"Yes, that would have been fun," I say.

"I once met Mickey Mantle at that place," says Big E.

I'm sure this is bullshit. "That must have been amazing."

"It was." Big E proceeds to tell me the details of the night he met Mickey Mantle at Shea O'Malley's, and I act as interested as I can. My eyes throw darts of *Yes Yes Yes* back at him. This is the respectful thing to do. I repeat that in my head like a mantra.

When the coffee's done, I do up his cup the way he likes it: black, with a cane field's worth of sugar. I push the cup toward him and he wraps his huge palms around it. This makes me think of Kendall. Of sitting across from her earlier, watching her obliterate that poor coffee with creamer. And I get this sensation of *better*. I feel better about what happened between her and me that night last summer. The regret, the mortification, the need to make things okay with Eliza even though at the time I knew in my heart we were over.

So, what about this Random Acts of Kindness dare?

I know why it's so tempting. I feel the need to pay someone, or something, back for being a bystander. Maybe that was why I had the Eliza dream.

I will never, ever not be worried about her.

My damn fingers. There they go again, straight for her damn number on my damn phone. I go into the bathroom and shut the door.

"Hey," says Eliza when she picks up. It's her baseline voice. She could be doing anything and her voice wouldn't tip me off. Riding a horse, or reading the paper, or in the middle of sex.

"Just calling to see . . . how was your Christmas?" I can't tell her I had a dream that she was in trouble.

"Boring. The way I like it."

She doesn't have to explain to me. Boring means her parents aren't fighting. It means that her mom is still in AA.

"Did you see Eileen this week?" Eileen is her therapist. I feel like I need to ask. Like she still needs me to.

"Yes, sir," says Eliza. "I hear you're grandpa-sitting."

"You talked to Jamie?"

"Yeah, yesterday. He said he was headed into the city to hang out with you."

So he didn't tell her about Kendall. Thank God for some common sense.

I hear her draw in a breath. "I'd love to do that, too. Come in and see you. I miss your stupid face."

I miss her stupid face, too. Her enraging, bitchy, luminous face.

"Let's talk in a few days," I say. "If they can't find a new aide right away, I'll still be here."

Because where else will I go? I have nine months until

Brown. A giant empty basin to fill with something besides wasted time and possibilities.

"What about New Year's?" she asks. "If you're there, I should be there, too."

"I don't think that's a good idea."

"Too much baggage?"

"Uh, just a bit."

"Max, you don't own New York. You can't ban me from the city."

No, I can't ban her. I don't want to. What I want to do is spend New Year's Eve with her and not eating pickled herring and crackers in front of the TV, saying *yes* over and over again.

"I gotta go," I whisper, because it takes all my strength to resist her like this. "Talk to you soon."

We say good-bye. I take a deep breath. Then it comes, an understanding that glimmers in the growing light.

You idiot, says a voice inside me. *The dream was about Luna.*

Big E is ready to move back to his chair. I watch him walk, slowly and steadily. He doesn't want people putting their hands on him if not mortally necessary. I'm supposed to just watch him and be ready to . . . I don't know, call 911 if he falls? I have never felt so completely useless.

Once he's settled in, I hand him the remote. Fill up his water bottle.

"I'm going out for a walk," I say. "Call me if you need anything."

He doesn't answer because he's already focused on the TV.

I stuff my feet into my boots, grab my coat. Fly out of there faster than ever.

I'm halfway through the lobby when my phone rings. Kendall's name glows on the screen.

"Max?" she says when I answer.

"Hey!" I sound way, way too excited to hear from her. "Did you really score a kindness?"

She laughs. "I did." She proceeds to tell me about it. I wish I'd been there. I would have done the same. I think. I hope.

"Nice," I say. "One down, for sure."

"Listen, I have some news about Luna. She's alive."

"How do you know?"

"My brother's boyfriend is a journalist. He called the publicity people for all the nearby hospitals and cashed in a favor. But that's all they could tell him. Critical, but stable."

"That's great," I say.

"She could be in really bad shape."

"Let's focus on the positive."

"We may never know more than that."

"Not ideal, sure," I say. "But better than nothing."

"Yeah, I guess." Kendall sighs.

"Did you tell Jamie this news, too?" I ask. "He'll want to know."

"I left him a message."

Another silence. Ugh.

The next thing comes out of my mouth on its own, without my permission. I swear. "What are you doing right now?"

"Getting ready for dinner and a show with my mom. Why?"

"Do you have plans tomorrow?"

Kendall pauses. "No."

"Let's meet up."

Another pause. "Will you do this dare thing with me?"

"Sure." If it gets me out of the apartment, absolutely.

Kendall's quiet for a moment. I really want her to say yes. I don't want another day of hanging out by myself, because I suck at it.

"Okay," she finally says. "I know exactly where to go. Want to meet me on the corner of Park and Fiftieth Street?"

We figure out a time to meet, then hang up. This is good. I feel *better*.

Then I see a flash of Kendall's face from this morning. Freckles on her nose, auburn hair twirled around a finger, green eyes blinking slowly closed, then open.

I feel the blood flowing again.

God, I'm disturbed.

Kendall

"IT'S A CLOSET," SAYS MY MOTHER.

"It's a guest room *and* a closet," chirps Emerson. "A *Groset*. Hey, Andrew! I just came up with a new word!"

My brother moves off toward the kitchen, leaving Mom and me alone in the closet doorway. She gives me a dubious look, then steps all the way into the small space and sits on the bed. I can tell she's still angry with me from the way the corners of her mouth keep twitching.

"How is this better than being at home?" she asks, her voice a flat line.

"Uh, because it's in a city full of fun stuff to do? And I get to spend some time with Emerson. I won't see him much after I go back to school."

I prepared that argument and it seems to be a good one: Mom's expression warms up.

"Well, I'm glad you two are having fun together," she says. "Are you able to sleep in here?"

I'm about as able to sleep in here as I am anywhere else, which means not very able at all. I shrug, and Mom sighs because her Shrug-to-English language skills are excellent.

"Did you bring melatonin? Because I'll buy you some if you didn't."

"That would be great. Thanks." I try not to use the stuff if I don't have to, but sometimes I have to. Like tonight, when I know what Thought Worms will slither toward me when I close my eyes: Luna and the strangers and the sound of that bus with its brakes like a trumpeting elephant, and also Jamie and Max. Jamie in the museum and Max in the coffee shop. Oh, and that dad and his daughter, Sophie. I could go on. I usually do.

Mom's gaze settles on my suitcase, which feels like a third person in the room. "I'm still not sure why you didn't unpack when you first got home."

"I was busy Christmas shopping," I say, which is true but not a good enough reason and we both know it. How do I explain it to her when I can't explain it to myself?

"But certain things must be dirty."

"Aren't you glad Santa brought me new socks and underwear?"

My mother shakes her head and sighs again. I can tell she wants this to be a special night despite the annoyances of having this quirky and unpredictable daughter. "Well, you look nice," she says.

I'm wearing a vintage 1970s dress I bought at a flea market in Paris called Les Puces de Saint-Ouen. It's navy silk with tiny polka dots and a white belt. I got the dress thinking I'd wear it to school when I went back, because it's the kind of thing I always wished I could wear to school. But now that I have it on, I know there's no way. This looks like I'm trying to be someone else. Of course, everyone wants to be someone else, but you're not supposed to be obvious about it.

"Thanks," I say, and go to find my coat.

After we get to the restaurant, the hostess leads us to a booth which I'm pretty sure is the same one we sat in two years ago. This is a holiday tradition for Mom and me: early dinner and a Broadway show. Every year, even if we have family visiting or the weather is terrible. She always makes it happen. I really, really love that she does that, but of course I never tell her.

We sit, and my mother takes her napkin and opens it onto her lap, which reminds me to do the same.

"So what exactly have you been doing in the city?" she asks.

"I went to the Met yesterday," I reply, quickly curating my experiences over the last forty-eight hours. Mom nods in approval of this time well spent, and now that I've set things up nicely, I go in for the shot: "I'd like to stay for New Year's, if that's okay."

My mother's face sinks and she's about to say something I don't want to hear, but then a waiter comes over and introduces himself. She orders a glass of wine and I get a Shirley Temple, which is always my special-occasion drink, mostly just for the cherry.

"What's his name?" asks Mom after the waiter leaves.

"Whose name?" I ask, confused.

"Kendall," says Mom, actually rolling her eyes at me. "I've raised three sons. Two of whom were girl-crazy and the third of whom was boy-crazy. I know when there's something going on."

The problem with parents is that they can make the phrase *something going on* sound disgusting.

"It's Jamie, a guy I met last summer, and we kept in touch when I was away. We've become friends."

I try really hard to hide the excitement and hope in my voice, and probably fail.

It must be weird for my mom, me being almost eighteen with a zero balance on my dating record. Sullivan and Walker were demigods in high school. They had so many girls coming in and out of our house, I had a full makeup collection accumulated by the time I was twelve. Emerson's been a serial monogamist since ninth grade; he had boyfriends every year for a full year each, until sophomore year in college and meeting Andrew.

Fortunately, my mother had already passed on all her

advice about men to Emerson, so it was no big deal that I wasn't dating.

"Do you like boys or girls?" she asked me once when I was fourteen. Ari had just slept over and I was standing at the window, watching her car drive away.

"Boys, definitely," I'd said.

"It's okay if you like girls. Emerson cleared the way for you on that. Or if you like both, that's okay. It's also okay if you're not sure."

"*Mom.* Stop being so evolved. I like boys."

"I'm glad you know," she'd said, but then I could still see the next question hovering in her head like a comic book thought bubble. *Then where are the boys?*

Turns out, they were in Ireland. Or at least, one was. One named Declan who made soccer, I mean football jerseys look hot. One who saw our group staying at the local hostel and realized this was his chance to notch an American girl. He honed in on my friend Chloe first, when we were all hanging out at a pub, but his friend Daniel beat him to her. I was next in Declan's line of sight. Sometimes you're happy to be in the line at all.

If my mother were a different person or I were drinking a Monaco (beer and grenadine syrup; that's an alcoholic Euro-version of a Shirley Temple and sure, I drank those like soda), I would tell her about Declan and about the blanket on the grass on the hill. How Chloe wished she hadn't slept with Daniel but I didn't regret Declan. I knew it wasn't going to be the same as it is in movies, and besides, I liked it. I especially like that it's done and now I have some nice pictures of him in my phone.

The drinks come and we sip. I'm worried that she's going to ask me more about Jamie and I won't be able to tell her without spilling the story about Luna and I don't want to go there right now. Must deflect.

"So what did I miss at home the last few days?"

A shadow flickers across Mom's face and she sits up straight. For my mother, a good attitude always starts with better posture.

"Well, let's see," she says, placing her drink carefully on the table. "Walker had a big fight with Sully shortly after you kids left. Sully and Amy went back to Baltimore earlier than they'd planned. And Walker's been in his room ever since."

"Oh, Mom. I'm so sorry."

She shrugs. "That's Walker."

I could fill in the rest. That's Walker, my son who dropped out of college and still lives at home, working at a snack foods warehouse.

"He'll find his path," I say to my mom, and she nods, biting her lip. It's an empty cliché so I want to fill it with something real. "Aren't you glad I went away? So maybe I won't be like him?"

Real does not always equal comforting. My mother is crying a little now. I can actually be so stupid.

"Kendall," she says, dabbing her eyes with the corner of her napkin. "I am glad you went away. But you and Walker are different people."

Of course we are, but the ways we're alike—they're not good ones. Walker was diagnosed with ADHD when he was eight. It took them until I was twelve to figure it out, because I wasn't jumping on chairs or jabbing other kids in the crotch with pencils (my brother did that a lot). I wasn't hurting anyone and in fact I was doing the opposite, crying every night because somebody said something that hurt *me*. In the mornings, I didn't want to go to school, tired of trying so hard and failing so often, and knew I was the stupidest kid in the class. I fell further and further behind, especially with math or anything I had to memorize. They called me spacey, a daydreamer, scattered. Eventually there was a new word: *inattentive*, which explained things but didn't fix them.

Medication was a patchwork quilt of treatment for Walker. Something would help for a while, until it didn't. Sometimes it helped too much, turning him into a pleasant pod-person version of my brother. Eventually, he got in trouble for selling his pills to his friends. After everything they went through, my parents didn't want to reopen that Pandora's box with me. Maybe when I turn eighteen, I'll explore the medication thing for myself.

"Of course we're different people," I say.

"Yes," agrees Mom. "Different people, different paths."

Over here in Kendall-land, a Thought Worm bursts forward, toward the light.

If things work out with Jamie, it'll be a million times easier to go home and back to Fitzpatrick. I know it won't solve all my problems—I'm not *that* person, thank God—but I'll be part of something. As a girl with a boyfriend, I'll fit in better. But if things don't work out, maybe I don't have to go back yet . . . or at all. I can stay in the city with Emerson and Andrew. I can get a job to help them pay rent. I'll fix up the Groset real nice and get my GED. Emerson's a teacher! He can help me. I can still go to college, just later and on my own terms when I feel totally ready.

It'll be a smart move, a wise move, and won't be a form of procrastination at all, I swear.

Wicked is amazing, obviously. At intermission I flip through the *Playbill* and think of all the other ones I have at home. Mom comes back from the ladies' room and as she sinks into the red velvet seat next to me, I notice she's been crying again.

"I know the line was long down there, but it couldn't have been that traumatic," I joke.

This does make her laugh. "I was thinking as I was waiting," she says. "What you said before about the Movable School and not ending up like Walker. It was a no-brainer to send you, really. I know how hard it'll be for you to go back to Fitzpatrick."

It must be the *Wicked* effect. She's suddenly seeing me as Elphaba, complete with green skin and awkward witch's hat, a girl who doesn't belong anywhere.

This is my window: I can pitch the idea of staying with Emerson. We're all warm and fuzzy right now and even though she wouldn't agree to anything, a seed would be planted.

But the lights start to dim and Mom reaches out to squeeze my hand.

"Stay for New Year's," she says. "Make the most of it."

I squeeze back. That's the closest I'll get to saying the things I want and need to say to her, for now.

DECEMBER 29

Max

I WALK THE THIRTY-TWO BLOCKS DOWN PARK FROM
Big E's to Fiftieth Street, enjoying every step on the cold-but-sunny concrete. Aunt Suze is taking my place today, interviewing some poor unsuspecting home aide candidates. I'm so happy to be out of that apartment, I could weep.

There's Kendall, waiting on the corner.

"Hey," I say when she sees me.

"Hey," she says back.

So here we are again. Kendall examines the curb. I don't know what to do next. I can only hope we'll push through this horrible awkward phase and get to the normal-interaction part. The *better*.

"Should we walk toward Fifth?" I finally ask her. She nods. We start moving. "You said you wanted to go somewhere in particular, right?"

"Uh-huh. St. Patrick's. I want to light a candle for Luna."

This strikes me as a painfully lovely thought. I feel that pain in my chest.

"Also," Kendall continues, "it's packed around there this time of year. Should be plenty of opportunities for random acts of kindness."

"Both excellent ideas," I say. She smiles.

Silence again as we walk. Kendall stares hard at many of the people passing by. If the way we were connected wasn't twisted and weird, I'd ask her something along the lines of *What are you thinking about?*

Instead, the best I can do is: "You okay?"

She nods, then breaks out laughing.

"What?" I ask.

"So many people," she says, shaking her head. "It makes you wonder."

"Can you be more specific?"

"Well, pretty much everyone has two eyes, a nose, and a mouth, right? How can there be so many variations, that each person has a completely unique face?"

I scan the folks walking past us. There are a lot of them since the sidewalks are much more crowded with tourists here. Their faces are every size, shape, color. Built with the same basic materials, but each one so different. I'd never considered it before.

"Yeah, that's intense."

We fall back into the quiet. Kendall takes a deep breath, and it occurs to me that she's as uncomfortable with these lulls as I am. We could have an awkward-silence-filling smackdown.

"Also," she continues, "isn't it weird to think that for each person we see, sex happened?"

"Beg your pardon?"

Kendall doesn't turn to notice the surprise on my face, the flush of embarrassment. "Sometimes I look around and all I see is sex," she says, with dead seriousness. "Instead of a person in clothing walking around, I see two people naked and doing it."

I follow her gaze to an old man slouching his way down the other side of the street. Then the picture comes into my head: two nameless, faceless people having sex. Probably a long, long time ago. But still.

"That is really disturbing," I say.

"I know, right?" she says, cracking up again. Her laughter jingles. "Sometimes it's fun to disturb yourself."

She stops, steps out of the flow of foot traffic. Takes out a notebook and leans against a building. Writes something down. I catch a glimpse and all I see is *MORTY, age 82.*

"Who's Morty?" I ask.

Kendall shrugs. "A name I just came up with for that elderly guy. I'm collecting characters for a novel I'm working on." She holds up her notebook and flips through the pages. Each page has a name and a person sketched out. Some written notes. They look a bit like manga characters. She's a really good artist.

I say, "I didn't know you were a writer. I thought you were into photography, like Jamie."

She shrugs and her demeanor changes, as if *this* is the thing that actually embarrasses her. Not admitting that when she looks at people, all she sees is sex. "I used to be. I've sort of moved on. It's a bad habit, jumping from interest to interest. But this book is different. I'm committed."

We're quiet again. I hear people speaking French behind us. To our left, a woman has a thick Southern drawl.

"So what exactly are we looking for?" Kendall asks. "One thing I discovered yesterday is that it's harder than you think, knowing when a complete stranger needs your help."

"You did okay with that little girl at the store."

"Lucky break," she says.

Up ahead, there's a woman with a tiny dog on a leash. It stops to sniff around the base of a potted tree, then assumes the position.

"We could offer to scoop that dog's poop," I suggest.

"Would that really make a difference?" asks Kendall.

I shrug. "Who knows. Maybe she's having the worst possible day, and picking up that poop would push her over the edge."

"Okay. Go for it."

"You're the girl," I say. "If I offer, she'll think I'm creepy."

Kendall shakes her head and rolls her eyes, but I can tell she knows I'm right. Girls rarely think about how guys need to balance the creepy factor in all their social interactions. Especially for someone like tall-and-bony me. I spend most of my life trying not to seem nefarious.

As the woman shakes out a plastic bag, Kendall steels herself with a deep breath. Steps up to the woman.

"Would you like me to do that for you?" she asks with a vague gesture toward the fresh pile of dog shit.

The woman gives Kendall a horrified look. "What? Why?"

"Just because." Kendall glances nervously at me. "Just to be nice?"

The woman takes a step away from Kendall. So does the dog. "No, thanks. I'm good."

Kendall comes back, looking completely dejected. "Wow," she mutters.

I watch the woman put a plastic shopping bag over her hand and pick up the poop, then invert the bag so it's hermetically sealed like something toxic. Or precious. She glares at us, thoroughly weirded out.

"Don't take it personally," I say to Kendall. "Nobody's used to offers like that."

"You said real kindness was easy," Kendall reminds me. "*You just have to do it.*" She mimics me with a deep, dumb voice.

I have to laugh. "Okay, so I was an idiot. I usually am. Should we call the whole thing off?"

"No," she says, with determination. "I liked how that felt, yesterday with the little girl. Maybe we should aim lower."

"Not seven random acts of kindness?"

"Maybe not seven *each*. Erica didn't specify that, did she?" Kendall pauses, tapping her bottom lip with a red-gloved finger. "Seven total? If we work together?"

The word *together* hangs there between us, offering more than three syllables' worth of meaning. It means spending time with each other. It means that maybe we're friends.

We reach the corner of Fiftieth and Madison. While we're waiting for the light to change, Kendall's phone dings. She glances at it, then pulls the screen closer. Squints. Confused. After a second, she makes a face and recoils from her own device.

"Ew!"

"What? What is it?"

"My brother," she says, shaking her head. "My brother just texted me the weirdest message."

Her cheeks flush again. She holds the phone out to me. I'm almost afraid to look.

It's a photo of a young guy, shirtless and smiling. Wow. He looks pretty good. I need to start working out. Underneath it is the message: **Hey Brian, looking forward to later.**

"That's your brother?" I ask. Kendall nods, clenching her eyes shut. "Your brother just sent you a flirting selfie by accident?" She nods again. I bust out laughing. Come on, it's hilarious.

But Kendall's giving me a dirty, dirty look. "You don't understand. Emerson has an Andrew, not a Brian. They live together."

I shut myself up. "Oh."

She gives her phone the same withering look she gave me. "This doesn't make sense."

"Are you going to respond?"

"I might throw up."

"Don't throw up."

We have the light now. I reach out and put my hand gently on her back. It's an instinctive move. If I pull away suddenly, it'll be even more awkward. *Go with it, Max.*

"Let's cross," I say, and Kendall lets me guide her forward.

Kendall

WHEN WE REACH THE OTHER SIDE OF MADISON
Avenue, Max stops dead.

There's a guy sitting cross-legged on a blanket spread out on the corner, his back against the granite of a building. Long hair in dreadlocks, multiple layers of dirty clothes, torn work boots. An empty coffee can sits in front of him, along with a sign that says: HUNGRY HOMELESS VET. GOD BLESS.

"It's happening!" yells the guy. "You don't know! Because you don't ask! That's what they're counting on! But I can tell you, it's happening and it's going to change things for all of us!"

An older woman pauses in front of the blanket, fishes a dollar bill out of her purse, drops it in the coffee can.

"I'll give you all the information you're going to need," the homeless guy tells the woman with a mix of gratitude and excitement.

The woman holds up her hand and shakes it in a *No, thanks* gesture. She smiles politely at him, then speeds up her pace.

Max frowns as he watches the woman hurry away. I see the wheels turning in his head and although I don't know what they're churning up, I say, "You know he's not really a vet, right? Or religious. I think these guys do market research on what signs get them the most money."

"Yeah, I know all that," he says.

"Also I read an article about some dude who does this and earns thousands of dollars a month."

"I saw that article, too."

"And remember, we have that no-money rule. . . ."

"*Yes!*" he practically hisses at me.

"So what are we doing here?"

"Not sure," says Max, who hasn't taken his eyes off the guy. "I just thought . . . what if we listen to what he's saying? Nobody else is."

"Because what he's saying is crazy?"

Max gives me a sideways, twinkle-eyed glance. "Are you sure?"

We both stare at the "homeless vet," who in turn is staring at the ground as people walk by. He seems to be very interested in everyone's feet. I guess that's a tricky thing for him, deciding where to look. It's not like he can fiddle with his phone or read a magazine.

Finally, Max steps forward and sinks into a squat next to the guy.

"Hi," says Max. "I'm Max."

The guy looks at him. Offers a hand wearing two gloves, one on top of the other. They're both see-through thin. "Josh," says the guy. "What up?"

Huh. I would not have pegged him for a Josh. A Ronald, maybe, or Horatio, something like that. I'm already thinking about how to sketch him.

"What is it that's happening?" asks Max. "What don't they want us to ask about?"

The guy pauses, regards Max cautiously, and frankly I can't blame him. "The cameras," he says. I guess I should call him Josh.

"What cameras?" I ask, stepping closer to them.

"The tiny ones on every single building," Josh says, pointing up and around us. "On every car. Every street sign. Fire hydrants. Mailboxes. Trees. Traffic lights. Any place you can think of, they're there."

We're all quiet for a moment. I'm trying to think of what to say to that.

"Who put them there?" asks Max.

"Private corporations. You'd think the government, right? But the corporations . . . they're the ones who have the most to gain from spying on everything we do. They want to know what we're wearing, eating, watching."

"I have to say," says Max, "if that's true, I don't really have a problem with it. I have nothing to hide. How is that different from the tons of consumer research that's being done on us all the time?"

"That's a good point," I add. "And sometimes security footage helps catch criminals."

"But it violates our rights," says Josh, looking at me, and his eyes are very clear. "Listen, I know about this stuff. I used to be in a long-range surveillance unit."

"So you *are* a vet," says Max.

"Nineteen months in Iraq."

"Where do you sleep?"

"At a shelter."

"Doesn't the VA help you?" Max presses.

Josh pauses. "It's a long story."

"What do you do with the money you take in during the day?" I ask. Max glares at me, but Josh breaks into a grin.

"I spend most of it on photocopies," he replies, and reaches into a duffel bag, taking out a homemade flyer, aka a letter-size sheet of yellow paper folded in half. He gives it to me, then pulls out another for Max.

Every inch of the front page is filled with handwritten poems.

I fumble to open the flyer with my gloves. Inside, more poems, some scrawled in print, some in cursive, all different sizes. It's hard to tell where one poem ends and another begins, but maybe that's the point. My eyes settle on one that's written larger than the others, the letters slanting sideways.

We fly into the night
Not knowing where we'll land
In the middle of a fight
Or in pieces on the sand

I glance over at Max, who's also reading. "Good stuff, man," he says to Josh.

A police officer breaks through the crowd.

"Every day you have to do this?" asks the officer.

Josh just shrugs, completely unfazed. "It's a great spot."

"It's an *illegal* spot."

Josh sighs, gets up, and starts collecting his things.

"Do you need us to call the shelter for you?" says the officer. The set of his jaw has softened and behind his face-swallowing wraparound sunglasses, I can tell there's some sympathy.

"No, no, sir," says Josh. "I have somewhere to be."

Josh steps off the blanket and picks up his sign, coffee can, and duffel bag. Max bends down to grab the blanket, folding it in half, then in quarters. He offers it to Josh and doesn't even seem to care that the thing looks saturated with filth. I'll offer him some hand sanitizer once we're on the next block.

"Thanks, kid," says Josh to Max, taking the blanket.

"No problem."

"I mean, thanks for stopping." His voice dips lower.

Max smiles. "You're welcome."

They both look at me. "Good luck," I say, and then wish I'd come up with something less stupid.

Josh moves toward the corner and disappears into a knot of people. When the knot untangles, he's gone. Max looks at me and I wish I knew him better so I knew what this look means.

"Do you think he's mad that we didn't give him any money?" I ask.

"Did he seem mad?"

"No."

"He seemed happy that we stopped, right? That we bothered to actually talk to him."

Happy is a strong word to use here, but maybe *un-sad*. Then I catch Max's drift.

"You're asking if this counts."

"I think it should totally count," says Max.

"How was that a random act of kindness?"

Max makes an exasperated sound. "How is it *not?*"

"I don't feel like we helped him. All we did was listen to him talk."

"Exactly!"

There's so much energy in Max's smile, it's hard not to take whatever it's offering.

I've walked by hundreds of these people. Not just in New York but at home, too. There's a guy who basically lives on

Main Street with his shopping cart and a pit bull named Lulu. Then, in Europe. So many that I really perfected the "looking away without feeling guilty" routine. I don't know what I feel when I think of all of them as a whole. But now I do know this one guy's name, and that he has ideas and writes poetry that's not terrible.

"Yeah," I say finally. "It counts."

"Two down," says Max.

"Two down," I echo. "But we didn't get a picture to prove this one."

"Erica will have to take our word for it, I guess. We do have his flyer."

I stop in my tracks. "Or I can record it another way. Hang on."

I step toward the wall of a building, take out my pen and notebook and prop it up against the cold stone. Then I slip off a glove so I can scribble Josh's name and where we met him, what we did. When I'm finished, I tuck everything back into my bag and tug the glove back on. It feels like I just wrote one page in a story.

We start walking toward Fifth again. My phone dings and I glance down, my heart jumping because maybe it's a message from Jamie. But it's from Emerson.

I think I may have sent you a text meant for someone else.

I stop for just a second, keeping Max's tall head in the corner of my eye.

You did, I reply.

There's a pause. Then:

Shit fuck dammit dammit dammit. Call me.

OK but later, I type back. **In the middle of something.**

Um, yeah, that's putting it mildly.

Josh

Alone in the middle of thousands
Me and myself are best buddies
Together against our

UH. SHIT. I CROSS THAT LAST LINE OUT.

Been having a bitch of a time figuring out the rest, because there are no good rhymes for "thousands." I tried "hundreds" and "millions" but those don't work either. Yeah, I know poems don't have to rhyme but that's my thing. In the service, I was known for my rap skills. It's not the rhyme so much as the rhythm.

129

My days have rhythm, too.

The beats are goals:

Make as much cash as I can before I get booted from my spot.

Eat some protein.

Try to stay gluten-free even when the only thing you find in the garbage is a giant piece of Italian bread. With butter.

Keep myself hydrated without resorting to the water from the public bathroom sink that says "not suitable for drinking."

Don't urinate in public even when you have to piss like a racehorse.

Resist the urge to call home.

Resist the memory of my mom's voice urging me to call home.

Go to the Veteran Service Unit and get back on meds.

I'm able to do all of these things except the last one. But I keep it in the goals, part of the rhythm, so that must mean something.

Those kids.

They stopped.

I'm probably something they have to write a school assignment about. Or a story for their friends.

Know what? I would be fine with that.

Go ahead, tall guy and redheaded girl. Tell the story. Pass along what I said about the cameras, and it's okay if your buddies laugh as long as it crawls into their ears and curls up in their brains. Because someday they'll remember, and what they'll remember is that I was right.

Then wherever I am, even if I finally ditched the idea of being alive, I won't be gone.

Max

WE STEP INTO ST. PATRICK'S CATHEDRAL THROUGH
the side entrance on Fiftieth. No sanctuary from the crowds
in here. It's even more packed than the street. People shuffle
through the aisles and slump in the pews, checking their cell
phones. But if I look up, toward the soaring buttressed ceiling
and the stained-glass windows, all that falls away. Being Jewish
doesn't mean I can't appreciate a dazzling house of God.

Kendall tugs my sleeve and cocks her head toward a woman
sitting by herself in a pew. The woman's eyes are closed and
she's taking deep, in-through-your-nose-out-through-your-
mouth breaths.

"What do you think she's thinking about?" Kendall

whispers. The woman bends forward, planting her forehead into her palms. "My guess is, her marriage falling apart."

"Wow, you went straight there, huh? What if she simply has a headache?"

"Boring."

"Yeah, well, some people are. We don't all deserve to be characters in your novel."

Kendall's face falls. Shit. I've hurt her feelings.

"I didn't mean . . . ," I say.

"It's okay. You just reminded me of something Jamie said the other day, that every moment is full of stories."

This feels weird, for her to bring up Jamie right now. But of course, why wouldn't she? Besides, I've heard Jamie say that, too.

Kendall tugs my sleeve again and pulls me to the right, deeper toward the heart of the cathedral. We pass one altar, then another. Then she stops.

"This is the one," she says.

There are two stands full of lit candles, and between them a bronze statue of St. Theresa waits there, watching. I'm not sure if she's supposed to inspire guilt or hope. Maybe both. (Could be an effective combination, actually.)

The donation box asks for two dollars, and I get the sense the honor system works pretty well here. I dig two dollar bills out of my pocket and slip them in the box. Pick a white candle and drop it into one of the empty blue glass holders. Grab a lighting stick and touch it to a candle that's already burning, then set mine aflame.

This one's for my grandmother.

I really miss you, Nanny. You would have loved all the holiday decorations in the city this year. Also, Big E is being extra jerky. Can you give us some suggestions on that?

After I extinguish my stick in a foam-filled box, I look up to see Kendall counting out some coins in the palm of her hand.

"I have a dollar bill plus eighty-seven cents," she says.

"I'm sure management will spot you the difference."

Kendall stuffs the money in the slot. She winces each time a coin lands and makes a noise. Nobody else seems to notice, though. Then she grabs a candle and a lighting stick. Surveys the holders. Like it matters which one she chooses. She takes a step to the right and bumps into a boy. He's maybe ten.

"Oh! I'm sorry!" says Kendall.

"It's okay," says the boy. He's staring at the candles. They light up unmistakable tears in his eyes.

"Are you all right?" I ask him.

"Where are your adults?" Kendall adds. This is, of course, the more appropriate question.

"My mom's right there," says the boy, pointing to a woman in the nearest pew. She's hunched over her phone. "We just came in so she could write an email."

The kid stares at the candles again.

"Are you going to light one?" Kendall asks.

The boy shakes his head. "I wanted to. For my dad. But Mom won't give me the money if it's for him."

Kendall looks at me with a raised eyebrow. It's funny that

we already have this language. I don't know her at all, really. But damn if I don't know what she's thinking.

Kendall glances at the mom, who's still engrossed in her correspondence. Then she offers the stick to the boy.

"Here. I paid for that candle. I want you to have it."

The boy bites his lip and shakes his head. He's got long bangs that fall across his face. He looks up shyly through them. "My dad's not dead. He's just . . . gone."

We're silent a moment. Processing what that might mean. Could be a hundred different things that are all pretty much the same.

"Sometimes gone is worse than dead," says Kendall with a nod. "Take it. Quickly, before she sees."

He glances furtively at his mom again. Grabs the stick. Lights it from the closest candle. Touches the flame to the fresh one. It takes slowly. At first, I'm worried it'll just die out and the symbolism will be too much to bear. But then the flame grows and the whole thing blazes.

"Nice job," says Kendall as he hands her back the stick.

The boy stares at the candle he lit. His features settle into something like relief. He takes a deep breath.

"Winston?"

Here comes Mom. She puts her hands on his shoulders. I was all prepared to hate her. Now that I see her face . . . well, I can't. She looks loving, but spent.

"Come on, sweetie," she says, and takes his hand. He lets her. As she leads him away, I keep waiting for him to look back at us. Flash a smile. Mouth the words "thank you." Anything. Come on, kid. Give us whatever you've got.

But they're gone.

"That was good," says Kendall as she stares at the flame.

It takes me a few seconds. "Oh. You want that to count."

She gives me an exasperated look like I'm ten, too. "I am not going to have this argument with you every time one of us does something. Of course it counts!"

"Maybe his father's a criminal. Or just the world's biggest asshole. What if the kid needs to let him go and we stopped him from doing that?"

Kendall shrugs. "Could be." She bites her lip, staring at St. Theresa. I wish she hadn't insisted on this particular, high-pressure altar. "Could be that doing this *helped* him let his father go. We'll never know. But did you see the expression on his face? It meant something to him. That's all that matters."

She's so sure. What choice do I have but to believe it, too?

Winston

THE CANDLE BURNS, AND THE FIRST THING IT REMINDS
me of is Dad's cigarette lighter.

He used that lighter on the fire pit in our backyard. This
past summer, he was finally going to let me do it. He said I was
old enough.

His friends in lawn chairs around the pit. Some of them
smoking, and not just cigarettes. Dad never did that. At least,
not when I was there. They take out their guitars and they sing
and they beg me to join in. I say no, I don't know the words.
Except of course I do.

The candle burns, and I imagine him feeling the heat wherever he is. Catching it flicker out of the corner of his eye. When

he turns to look, there's nothing there. But he knows what it means.

Winston's still here.

Mom says I won't understand. Mom says she'll explain more when I'm older. Mom says all I need to know is that she loves me and she'll never, ever leave.

She treats me like I'm eight, not eleven. She thinks I don't read her text messages and emails on her phone when she's left it in the bathroom, even though she's always leaving it in the bathroom. I mean, duh, of course I'm going to read them. She uses a lot of really inappropriate words on that phone, mostly talking about my dad. She needs to wash her own mouth out with soap.

He's gone and it's best not to think about him, Mom says, but those sound like inappropriate words, too. She can keep me from him now, but someday, that won't work anymore. Already she has trouble hugging me normally because I'm getting so tall.

I walk three steps behind her down the street toward the subway. Back to Staten Island we go.

The candle burns, even when it doesn't because maybe they put out all the flames before the cathedral closes up for the night.

The candle burns, so I'll keep my memories burning, too.

Kendall

WE PRESS OUR WAY TO THE BACK OF THE CATHEDRAL,
past the souvenir shop, and eventually out to the steps facing
Fifth Avenue. Across the street, there are actually barricades
to contain all the people fighting their way toward Rockefeller
Center.

Max pauses on the top step, looking terrified.

"Are you afraid of crowds?" I ask.

"Crowds are no problem for me. I'm a tower. I'm worried
about you."

"Because I'm not tall?"

"Because . . ." Max pauses again. "You know something? I

have no idea why I'm worried. Eliza always got freaked out by crowds."

"Well, she's tiny." A quick mini-fantasy unreels in my mind. Eliza under the feet of a stampeding crowd, and nobody can hear her screams. As mini-fantasies go, this one's really gratifying.

"And she's Eliza," he says. Which clearly means something specific to him, completely different from what it means to me. "Mostly I just worry. About everyone."

"I'm tougher than I look," I say, pretty sure that's true.

Max stares at me for a moment and then grins. "Okay, then. Where are we headed?"

I look to see which direction is less congested. "This way," I say, pointing uptown. "Central Park Zoo."

"Yes, ma'am." He offers his hand and I take it and try not to overthink this interaction but fail miserably. *Would Jamie freak out if he saw this?* asks a new Thought Worm.

We're friends, Thought Worm. Grow up already.

Once we're walking, Max lets go of my hand, and we travel in silence for a block. Then he says, "So, when you see lots of people in one place, you see multiple instances of copulation, right?"

"You make it sound soooo hot."

He laughs. I like making people laugh, but I like it extra with Max. This is definitely a boy who needs to smile more.

"Well," he says. "I see potential future-me's." He points to a guy a few paces in front of us, wearing a long camel-colored overcoat and a black leather man-purse, and whispers, "I could end up as him, for instance. I wonder what I do for a living where I need a bag like that."

"With a bag like that, I'd lay bets you're still single."

"You do one," Max says, elbowing me.

I scan the sidewalk and nod toward a woman with a tight ponytail and expensive stroller. "I could be her," I say. "Parenthood would be cool. Although that stroller freaks me out. It looks like it should be protecting an alien egg, not a human baby."

Max snorts, then stops to avoid walking into a guy coming out of a deli. Beard, mustache, glasses, wool beanie, plaid shirt, down vest, huge coffee drink. Max shoots me a sideways glance.

"God, no," I say. "Please don't be a hipster."

"Can I at least have a standard coffee order?"

"Fine. Something simple and classic, though. Cream and sugar. No fancy-pants."

"You've thought about this," says Max.

"Europe," I say by way of explanation. "I'm a café au lait."

Max smiles. He tilts his head as if he's trying to see me from a different angle, as if a forty-degree adjustment might show him something new. Then he starts walking again, I follow, and he says, "Tell me something about your trip."

I think for a moment. "We learned about architecture when we visited the Eiffel Tower. Then we had a contest to design and build one ourselves out of recycled materials."

"You packed a lot of experiences into a few months," he says softly, his voice sounding like it's coming from far away.

"Maybe in college you can spend a semester abroad."

"Yeah. Maybe."

I've talked a lot about me and now I want to give him a turn.

"Brown's a tough school to get into. You must be pretty psyched."

Max shrugs, like it was something that happened by accident. *Oops! I slipped and fell and applied to an Ivy League school and they accepted me.* I can tell he prefers to downplay how ridiculously smart he must be, and he doesn't even know my baggage. It takes me forever to do a single homework assignment. It doesn't matter how many people talk to you about learning differences, that everyone learns at their own pace. It's fucking embarrassing.

Max also doesn't know I once wanted to go to his school, where kids plan out their own learning. *"All the weirdos go there,"* said Emerson once, when someone mentioned the place, and all I could think was *maybe all the weirdos are waiting for me to join them.* Before I even met all these Dashwood people, I'd done my own research on it. I wanted to transfer so I printed out pages and pages from the Dashwood website. I begged my parents, shoving the papers into their hands. But they couldn't buy into the "democratic school" philosophy, couldn't believe that kind of freedom would work for someone like me, who had to be reminded three times every night to brush her teeth.

Then my mother found out about the Movable School and how I could spend a semester of hands-on learning, and still get high school credit for it. It seemed like a great compromise at the time, but now that it's over, I wish I didn't feel as if I was standing on the edge of a cliff.

We stop to wait for a light to change. I put my toes on the tip of the curb and look down and think maybe a cliff is no different than a street corner. Sometimes you just have to take a step, and sometimes you have to take a leap, and either way, all that really matters is that you're not standing still.

Max

"THANKS," SAYS KENDALL AS I HAND HER A TICKET
for the Central Park Zoo. "I'll pay you back."

"Don't worry about it. It's my treat."

I earned a more-than-decent salary at my demeaning job these last four months. What else am I going to spend it on? Oh, yeah. College. But right now, this seems more important.

We go through the admission gate and hang a quick right turn toward the sea lions. Kendall picks up her pace and rushes toward the railing. There's a sea lion swimming flips under the water.

"Hi!" Kendall says to it. She crouches so she can see the sea lion through the glass. Then she waves and it locks its huge cartoon eyes on her.

A memory comes over me. My grandmother and I watching the zookeepers throw fish at the sea lions. I'm holding her hand and she's got my sister on her hip.

"It's hard to feel down around sea lions," I say. One of them zooms out of the water, onto a rock. I'm sure it does this a hundred times a day but still, it looks joyful.

"*I* feel down," says Kendall softly, her eyes tracking the dark swimming shapes. "I'm sad that their enclosure is so small."

"I think most of these animals were born in captivity. Maybe they don't know any better. They don't know they're supposed to be wild."

"That makes it even sadder!"

I look at her face and realize, she feels things pretty deeply, this girl. That can't be fun.

"I know what you need," I say. "Follow me."

We move next door to the penguin house, which stinks. I mean, it actually stinks. Like bird shit and general *wildness*.

But that's not a big deal because, penguins. Kendall and I press our noses to the glass right at the waterline. The penguins dive and swim inches from our faces. I can't tell if Kendall's still sad.

"I wonder what they think of us," she says softly.

"Maybe they think we're the ones living behind glass. Maybe *they* feel sad for *us*."

Kendall's quiet for a few seconds. "They should."

I want to change the tone here so I say, "Hey, let's get a selfie with the penguins." I take out my phone. Before she has time to prepare, I pull her against the glass and crouch until I see both of our faces framed on the screen. Wait until a penguin is swimming by above our heads. Take the shot and show it to Kendall for approval. She looks confused, I look uncomfortable. Well, that perfectly captured the moment.

But she says, "Send me that," so I do.

Someone has been pressing against the back of my legs. I look down and there's a little girl, trying to get close to the glass. I step back to give her my excellent spot. Then I go lean against the wall on the other side of the room. I've been crazy tall since I was twelve years old. I've done that move countless times over the years. I don't even think about it anymore. I never count it as something that matters. It's an obligation, a responsibility I have to meet because I'm big. Actually, when I really think about it, it feels more like an apology than anything else.

After a few minutes, Kendall comes over. She leans against the wall next to me.

"Still feeling down?" I ask.

"What?"

"Did the penguins cheer you up or are you still pondering the ethical dilemmas of zoology?"

"Oh. I don't know." She seems surprised by this question, like she's already forgotten we talked about it. Five minutes ago. "I was making up a story about the penguins. See that big one on the iceberg thing? He's the penguin mafia boss."

I laugh. I can't help it.

"Do you write this stuff down?" I ask, nodding toward her purse and the notebook inside it.

"Sometimes, yeah. But sometimes it's just a story that lasts a few moments in my head. Honestly, if I wrote down every weird idea that ever crossed my mind, I wouldn't be able to function in normal life."

I've met other kids who talk this way. Self-aware. Conscious of what makes them different. I respect the hell out of that.

Kendall opens the zoo map and points to the tropical rain-forest building. "Let's go there now," she says.

So we do. The transition into this warm, humid space is jolting and terrific. I take off my coat. I'm about to offer my arm for Kendall's. But she folds it in half and ties it around her waist, so never mind.

Another memory. Me getting lost in this building on purpose. I'm wandering around, pretending I'm a jungle explorer. Hearing my grandmother call my name, frantic. Me liking it. Knowing they're looking for me. Knowing I'm missed.

Birds are squawking like they've always been squawking in here.

And somewhere, someone's crying.

I mean, not like in a metaphorical way. Someone nearby is actually crying. Bawling.

We round a corner and come upon a woman on a bench,

holding a flailing little girl. At first I think the kid is having some kind of seizure. That's how much flailing we're talking about. But the woman gets a slightly rough grip on her and speaks sternly.

"I'm sorry that happened but you cannot scream like this. You cannot!"

The woman's maybe in her sixties and the girl's about five years old. The girl's talking, but it doesn't sound like English. Or wait. Maybe it is. Tantrum-ese.

Kendall pulls me aside and gives me a quizzical look. She doesn't even have to say anything at this point. Everyone else in the tropical rainforest house is walking by, pretending they don't see or hear this *Exorcist* scene playing out in front of them. So of course we're going to stop and get involved.

Kendall steps near, but not too near, the bench and asks, "Is she okay? Do you need help?"

The woman looks at Kendall and her tight, annoyed face relaxes for a millisecond. Then it cinches up again.

"We're fine. Thank you."

"Are you sure?" prods Kendall.

"*Yes,*" the woman says. "We were here this morning and she bought a stuffed leopard from the gift shop. She left it here by accident, but when we came back to get it, it was gone."

"Someone took it!" yowls the girl.

"You checked Lost and Found?" I ask.

"Yes," sighs the woman, and her withering expression says, *Of course, you idiot.*

The kid's dressed like one of those American Girl dolls my sister used to collect. Shiny black shoes, white tights, pink wool coat.

"This is life, Charlotte," the woman says to the girl. "You lose things, other people find them. You have a hundred other stuffed animals at home." She glances at Kendall and me now. "Actually, more than that. Much more."

I can't get a read on whether this is a grandmother or a nanny. She's so bitchy, but probably because the kid is a brat. The kid's probably a brat because her parents are never around. We could be looking at a vicious cycle of overall nastiness here. To be honest, I'm relieved they don't need help.

But Kendall pushes. "If you only lost it this morning, maybe you could explain to the gift shop. Maybe they'd give you another one, just to be nice."

The woman laughs. Hard. Like she hasn't had a good laugh like that in a while. "Oh, honey, that is a lovely idea but I don't think so."

"Why not?" replies Kendall. "It can't hurt to ask. Look at all these tears." She points to Charlotte's pink, streaked face. The kid's a hot mess.

"No," says the woman. More firmly now. Even Charlotte shuts up and stares at her. "And you should mind your own business."

Kendall backs away and holds up her hands. "Okay," she says. "Hope your day gets better."

She tugs on my arm and drags me around the curve of the

path so we can't see them anymore. Then she stops. Her eyes are glassy.

"That's why," says Kendall, dabbing a tear. "That's why people don't get involved."

"Because someone might be mean and say, 'Mind your own business'?"

"It feels shitty."

"I agree. But sometimes you have to take the risk anyway."

"On an intellectual level, yes. Duh. But in the moment, you just react. You stay in your bubble. It's an anti-shittiness defense mechanism."

She's got a point. "So how do you break through that?" I ask. "I mean, we've been trying because of Erica's dare. But what about a non-dare situation?"

Kendall stares at a lemur. It stares back at us. It looks alarmingly like Big E, with the white hair and jaded expression.

"I don't know," she says. "I guess that's the point of the dare in the first place."

The lemur leaps from one branch to another. Kendall watches it move. I watch her.

She's deflating. I won't let that happen. "So," I say, pointing a thumb at the lemur-grandpa. "In the zoo mafia, who's this guy? Consigliere?"

Her nose twitches.

"No," she says with the hint of a smile. "He's the best hit man they've got."

Cora

I'VE BEEN A MOTHER FOR THIRTY-EIGHT YEARS, AND a grandmother for ten. I've seen a lot of terrible children. Trust me, this one's not the worst. Not by far.

This one, I've seen her spread some sunshine. Honest, real sunshine that comes from the well she has inside. But the odds are against her. Her father—my baby boy—is home maybe one night out of ten. Her mother works twelve-hour days. There are times it's after nine o'clock when I get home to the apartment they bought for me, just five blocks away.

My apartment with the fireplace and the bay window where I can read historical novels. My very own space for the first time in my life. Caring for Charlotte is a small price to pay in exchange for this. My son wanted his daughter to be raised by a family member, not a nanny. My son's very, very good at making deals.

That's how he got to own a penthouse with so many rooms; there are three extra they have no idea what to do with. They're empty right now. One of them, they're turning into a dance studio for Charlotte. Someone's coming next week to install the mirrors and a barre.

I will make a confession: I knew she'd left the leopard in the rainforest house. After thirty-eight years, I have a sense for when something is not as it should be. As we walked out and I noticed Charlotte did not have the animal in her arms, I looked back to see it sitting there on the bench.

It looked strangely free. Unowned. I found myself jealous of it for a moment. Then I turned away and kept walking.

Even knowing how much she'd carry on when she realized she'd lost it, it felt wonderful to keep walking.

This child needs nothing. This child needs to know what loss feels like. This child needs to know the rules that apply to everyone apply to her, too. Those rules aren't fair. But on the whole, she got the good end of that fairness. She'll be okay with the bad end every once in a while.

I know I looked so cruel to those kids.

I'm fine with them only seeing that part of the story.

Kendall

WE'RE STANDING OUTSIDE THE ZOO ENTRANCE ON
Fifth Avenue when Max's phone buzzes.

"I should get back," he says as he glances at it. "Do you want
me to walk you to your brother's?"

"No, I'll be okay." I probably won't. Because *my brother* is at
my brother's place and he'll want to talk about That Text. "I'm
going to hang out in the park for a little while."

Max nods and we stand there for what feels like ten minutes
but is really maybe three seconds. Finally he says, "I'll call you
later. Maybe we can meet up again tomorrow?"

"Sure," I say.

He takes a few steps backward, then raises his hand in a wave. I mirror him.

He turns to walk away, then stops and turns back for a moment.

"Three down!" he calls.

"What?"

"Three down! Four to go!"

I flash him a thumbs-up, and then he's gone.

I wish he weren't, and then I feel weird about that wish, and then decide it's just because I want someone there. I switch my wish to being at the zoo with Jamie. He would have taken some great photos of the animals and maybe we would have kissed in front of a red panda.

I head back into the park and spend a long time wandering aimlessly around, following one path into another, finding more characters for my book. I can tell there's snow coming, because the sky looks pale and guilty, like it's apologizing for what it's about to do. Eventually I start heading back to the apartment. My feet hurt and it's getting colder, and the Groset's looking extra cozy right now.

When are you coming home? texts Emerson.

On my way, I reply.

When I get to his block, he's waiting for me outside the building, a cigarette in one hand. He doesn't smoke.

"Hi?" I say, and it really does come out that way, with the question mark.

Emerson grabs my wrist and steers me around the corner,

then drops the cigarette, stubs it out with his snow boot. "For the record," he says, pointing to the butt, "this is something I do very occasionally in times of stress or awkward social situations."

"Okay."

"I am so embarrassed, I don't know what to say. Even to you."

I try to block out the image of that seductive selfie but nope, it's something I can't ever un-see. We're silent for a few moments until I realize he wants me to be the one to ask.

Fine. "Who's Brian?"

Emerson winces, closes his eyes.

"A guy I met a few weeks ago. He doesn't know I'm in a relationship." He opens one eye to peer at me. "What are you thinking about me right now?"

"I don't understand. Are you and Andrew having trouble?"

"No, not at all." He sounds a little disappointed about this.

"Everything does seem perfect with you guys."

"That's the problem!" Em sighs, shakes his head. Paces a little circle in front of me. "Andrew's got it all figured out. He wants us to get married, have kids, buy a house, the whole package. He says he's sure, but really, how can he be sure? We met when we were nineteen! I adore him. I'm so happy that I found him. But he also scares the crap out of me."

Okay, I know what's going on here. It's a pattern with my brother: he never knows how lucky he is, and he never sees what he has. In high school, he was the honor roll student, soccer team captain, guy with a million friends. And he spent most of that time complaining that he was never smart enough, fast enough, popular enough. I have fantasized about slapping him on many occasions and this should be one of them, but he's looking so confused right now.

"You should talk to him," I say.

"I can't. He gets really hurt when I bring up questions like this."

"You're right. Cheating on him is so much better."

"I haven't cheated on anyone yet. I've just been . . . flirting."

"But you're planning to hook up," I say. Emerson bites his lip. "Admit it."

"I can't talk to him," he says, like this is some great excuse. Then he looks me over. "Wait. Maybe you can."

"Pardon?"

"*You* talk to him. *You* tell him you're concerned about me, that I told you these things. He won't get defensive if it's you. He'll try to save face. But the seed will be planted and maybe we can have a real conversation about it."

I move away from him, down the sidewalk. "No, no, no. I am not getting involved with this."

"Come on, Kendall!" he says. "You owe me! We're putting you up in our guest room while you avoid your life."

"It's a *closet*."

"It's not Mom and Dad's."

He's got a point.

"Forget about owing or not owing," adds Emerson, his

features softening, his shoulders sagging. "It would just . . . help me a lot."

Help. The one word driving my day with Max, the point of our mission through a sea of strangers. Here is someone I love a lot, asking for it. Begging for it. And I actually said, *I am not getting involved.* There are many ways that's messed up, but I can't think about them right now. It's getting cold.

"And you won't meet up with this guy tonight?" I ask Em.

"I'll postpone."

"Postpone!"

He simply shrugs, as if that's supposed to explain everything. The one relationship in my life that I though: was healthy is in trouble for being *too healthy*, and now I have to fix that somehow.

"Okay," I say. "I'll talk to him."

"Thank you, Ken. You know I love you." He grabs my hand and starts kissing it.

"Whatever," I say, trying not to crack up. He's so charming and damn him for that.

Emerson hands me a twenty-dollar bill. "I'm going to the gym. Take Andrew out for coffee. He can't get all freaked out in public."

"Wait. I'm doing this right now?"

Emerson shrugs again, then turns and runs off down the street, his gym duffel flapping behind him.

Crap.

* * *

The barista calls Andrew's name and he gets up to grab our drinks. We're at a café called Dirt, which is really pushing the envelope of coffee-related names, don't you think?

He returns with two enormous cappuccinos, placing one in front of me. There's a white heart in the foam. I'm sure they do this for everyone but I take it as a message, and my eyes lock with Andrew's steel blue ones.

We're silent as we blow on our drinks.

There's a couple sitting next to us. They're in their fifties, I'm guessing, dressed for an adventure like hiking, perhaps, or climbing something tall, and look painfully out of place. They each have a cupcake and a mug, sitting across from each other while not talking. It's one of the saddest things I've seen all day, and I'm suddenly much more sympathetic to Emerson's situation.

"So," says Andrew. "Why did you want to take me out for coffee?"

Andrew's no dummy.

"I'm concerned about my brother," I say, pretending I'm a person who has not been talking to said brother about his state of unhappiness, but rather spends her days reflecting on the well-being of her loved ones.

Andrew nods. He doesn't seem surprised, and this surprises me.

"Me, too," he says. "He's been really on edge lately."

"Did he say why?" I prod.

"Some vague stuff about his job."

Ugh, this is going to be really tricky.

"Why?" continues Andrew. "Did he say something to you?"

I know my line here, and I need to simply say it. "Yes."

Before my very eyes, Andrew goes pale.

"Tell me," he says.

I take a deep breath. This should be easy, because I'm not lying. He did say something and all I have to do is repeat it.

"He's scared," I begin. "About the future. Your future, together. He loves you but . . . maybe everything feels a little too settled, too soon."

Andrew stares at me with those male model eyes again. Why am I doing this? Why am I helping my brother potentially throw away this guy? I want to chastely run my fingers through his blond hair and he might let me, if I don't piss him off.

"Too soon," he echoes, then swallows hard and drops his head. Oh God, this is crushing him.

"But he loves you so much!" I add.

Andrew raises his head again. He doesn't look upset, but . . . relieved. "I know exactly how he feels," he says, then takes a deep breath and leans back.

"You do?"

"I'm scared to death."

"Emerson thinks you have it all planned out. That you know what you want."

"There are times where I believe that. But then, there are times when I don't. We met when we were nineteen!"

"Okay, you two have to talk about this. My brother thinks you don't want to hear it."

"I don't."

"But you sort of have to."

Andrew nods and reaches across the table, takes my wrists. What is it with these guys and my wrists?

"Thank you, Kendall."

He's giving me more credit than I deserve, but I'll take it. I'm here, aren't I? I picture Max in the corner over there, his arms folded across his body, shaking his head. *Don't think for a moment that this counts.* No, it doesn't count in Erica's dare. But it counts somewhere more important.

"You're like the sister I always wished I had," adds Andrew, taking a sip of his drink.

"But you do have a sister."

"Exactly."

We both laugh. Whew. Mood's much better now. "I've already got three brothers, what's one more. You've got the gig," I tell him. "Just don't send me any sexy selfies by accident."

Andrew frowns and puts down his huge mug.

Oh. Yeah. That was a weird thing for me to say.

"What do you mean?" he asks.

"Nothing," I say. "Stupid joke."

He looks at me and damn it, those eyes again. "No, it wasn't. Who sent you sexy selfies by accident? Walker?"

It would definitely be easy to stick this on my brother Walker. He'd never find out he'd been accused and even if he did, he'd probably assume it was something that happened while he was stoned. But I came here to help not only Emerson, but Andrew, too. I don't want to lie to him.

"No," I say slowly. "It was Em."

Andrew leans in. Turns the eyes up to full volume. "Was he trying to send the pictures to *me*?" he asks, even though it's clear he knows the answer.

I shake my head no.

I'm sitting on the stairs outside the apartment door, and I can still hear Andrew and Emerson. They're not yelling, but there's so much in their voices. Not volume, just intensity, and let me tell you intensity burns your ears in a totally different way.

At least out here, I can't make out the actual words of what they're saying.

I hug my knees to my chest and lean my head against the stairway railing, whose black metal spokes look (and feel) way too much like prison bars. Mental note: next time you're coerced into relationship intervention, make sure you have somewhere to be right afterward.

Also, don't be an idiot and say something you're not supposed to. That'll be a bonus.

I have to get out of here.

Out on the street, it's colder than it was. Mom texted me earlier to make sure I knew that *tons of snow was coming*. There's definitely limbo in the air, that feeling of transition from one state of something to another. It feels exciting. Is it okay that it feels exciting? It looks like every person I pass is carrying a grocery bag full of bread, milk, and batteries. That deli over there has bare shelves, I can see them through the window.

What will I do if I can't blow off high school to Groset-squat in the city because Emerson and Andrew have split up?

So in the moment and in general with my life, I have no idea where to go or what to do. I walk more quickly, faking it until I'm making it, as if I knew both of these things with absolute certainty. Giant flakes of snow have started falling. They're taking the long, slow way to the pavement, each one whirling in the wind like it knows this is the last hurrah. I see fewer people on the street now, and maybe there's not a single loaf of bread, container of milk, or AA battery remaining on the Upper East Side.

After eighteen blocks, I turn back toward Emerson's place and text as I go. **Is it safe to come back?**

I stare at my phone, but there's no answer right away.

I end up at a Yum Yum Yogurt. One lone employee, a young woman, is slowly packing away the fresh fruit toppings into airtight containers. I fill a cup with a little bit of every flavor and use the rest of Emerson's coffee cash to pay for it, then shiver with every single bite.

Finally, my phone rings, except it's not Emerson's name on the screen.

Max.

"Hey," he says when I answer. "Calling to say that maybe we shouldn't meet up tomorrow, given the weather report."

"Yeah," I say. "You're probably right."

The employee drops a container and it crashes on the floor.

"What was that?" asks Max.

"Something fell. I'm at a fro-yo place on Lexington."

"What are you doing out? Isn't it snowing?"

"Eh, right now it's just fluffy and cinematic. There are some . . . domestic negotiations going on at my brother's and I don't want to go back there yet."

There's a pause.

"Do you want to stop by here to kill some time?"

"To your grandpa's?"

"You can meet him, then I'll walk you back."

The yogurt girl locks the door from the inside, so I can leave, but nobody else can come in. She turns to me and gives me a dagger-look.

"I'll be there in fifteen minutes," I say.

When the elevator doors open, Max is waiting for me in the hallway and I get the feeling I'm a sight for his sore eyes. Or maybe that's because he's a sight for mine.

"Come on in," he says brightly, leading me into the apartment. "I told my grandfather all about you."

I step inside and the first thing I notice is the smell. It's a rich smell, a combination of tobacco and wood and maybe some kind of spice. *Eau de Old Guy.*

"Let me take this," says Max as he lifts my coat from my shoulders and hangs it up on an iron rack with clawed feet.

"The news is saying over a foot now, but not until the early morning."

There's something strange about him, and I realize it's because I haven't seen him out of his parka in these last few days. He's wearing a half-zip pullover with a T-shirt underneath. The sleeves don't make it all the way to his wrists and his throat looks exposed, scarf-less. The fact that we're now spending time together sans outerwear seems like a big step.

"So, are you ready for the Ezra Levine experience?" asks Max.

"You make it sound like a Broadway show."

He smiles wickedly. "Winner of Ten Curmudgeon Awards, including Best Silent-But-Deadly Fart."

"You're so weird," I say, but I'm laughing.

I follow Max to what's next.

Max

THAT'S RIGHT. I ASKED THIS GIRL TO WALK HERE IN A
growing snowstorm so I don't have to spend any more time
alone with my grandfather. I'll make it up to the universe later,
I swear.

"Big E?" I ask as I knock on the wall of the living room,
where there's a black-and-white movie on TV. What I see of
my grandfather is motionless. Possibly asleep again.

I knock again, louder. Big E turns, sees me, and actually
grins. "Hey, champ."

"I brought a friend to meet you." I motion for Kendall to
step all the way into the room.

I watch Big E size her up. Twenty bucks, he says something about her hair.

"Hi," says Kendall. "I'm Kendall."

"A redhead!" says Big E. "Natural or out of a bottle?"

For the love of God. At least he didn't ask *Does the carpet match the drapes?*

Kendall's unfazed, though. "A hundred percent natural," she says proudly, with a smile.

Big E turns to me. "I always loved redheads. Jane Fonda. She was a juicy one."

"Uh-huh," I say. *Gross.*

He meets my eyes. "I don't blame girls for dyeing their hair that color."

"Me neither," I say softly, then glance at Kendall. She frowns. I didn't have time to explain the rule of Yes to her.

"What are you watching?" she asks Big E. On the screen, two guys drive an old car with a fake background going by.

"Some movie about brothers. I lost track of the plot."

A few painful minutes of us all watching the movie in silence. Okay, enough. I motion for Kendall to follow me back to the kitchen.

"Wow," is all she says.

"I know. He's pretty intense."

"No, I mean, wow, you just agree with everything he says."

"Well, yeah. He's sort of losing it."

"So?"

"So, you can't take him seriously."

"Why not?"

"Uh, because if I did, it would drive me crazy. Also, the guy's in a lot of pain, and he's angry and lonely. He deserves some slack, don't you think?"

Kendall considers this. Runs her pointer finger back and forth along the smooth granite of the countertops.

"Sure, of course he does. But you know who your grandfather reminds me of? That homeless guy on the street today."

"Josh," I say, super-glad that I remember his name.

"Josh," nods Kendall. "He's clearly losing it, too. He's sick. He was spouting nonsense. But you took the time to have a conversation with him."

"That's different."

"Is it? You made his day simply by taking him seriously. You made him feel heard."

"You don't think I'm making my grandfather feel heard?"

"Nope."

I'm a little pissed off now. She doesn't know anything about Big E. Or Nanny. Or our whole family.

"You haven't been here," I say, trying not to sound defensive. "Everything we do is to make him feel heard."

Kendall thinks for a moment, then shakes her head. "I don't buy that. When I'm talking to someone and they're just saying *yeah* and *uh-huh* and *right*, it's pretty clear they're not listening at all."

"Well, same here."

"So this is that."

"It's not."

Or is it?

I look at her. Her eyes are bright and mischievous. I take a breath to think about what she's saying. What I've been doing. What we've all been doing.

Oh my God. She's right.

"Oh my God," I say. "You're right."

Kendall lifts one corner of her mouth in a smile. It's a new kind of smile, one I haven't seen on her yet. Innocent but arrogant. Wendy crossed with Peter Pan.

"So what should I do?" I ask.

She thinks about this. Shrugs. "Not sure."

"You can't break this wide open without an alternative."

Kendall laughs. "Okay. How about you do the opposite of what you've been doing?"

"You mean, call him out on his bullshit."

There's the smile again, plus the eyes-on-fire. This girl kills me little by little. "Yes!" she says.

Calling Big E out on his bullshit is really appealing. Which feels so wrong. "I don't want to upset him."

"I'm sure he can handle it. He seems pretty tough."

As soon as she says that, I realize I'm full of crap. Because of course he's tough. Duh, he can handle it. We're not doing anything out of respect for his delicate feelings. I'm his yes-man because I'm terrified of the guy. We all are.

"Maxie!" bellows Big E from the other room.

"Go!" says Kendall, giving me a little push.

"You're coming with me!" I whisper-slash-beg.

We walk back toward the living room and I linger in the archway. Kendall gives me another push.

"Max!" he calls again.

"Hey," I say, walking into his line of sight. "What's up?"

"Suze was going to make me coffee, but she vanished."

"Suze left hours ago."

"Without saying good-bye?"

"You were asleep." The *S* sound for "sorry" forms in my mouth, but I silence it.

"Did she tell you about the parade of idiots that came through here?"

"Why do you think they're idiots?" I ask.

"Why?" he echoes.

"Did you talk to them long enough to gauge their intelligence level?" I smile, to let him know I'm not trying to be a dick. This is just a friendly challenge. Between a grandson and grandfather who aren't friendly at all.

Big E raises his eyebrows. "Maxie, I've lived a long time. I know when someone's an idiot."

"Well, Suze hired one of them to start in a few days."

"She *what*?"

Oh, crap. Sorry, Aunt Suze.

"Figures she'd run away without talking to me about this," sputters Big E.

I'm suddenly full of reasonable explanations. He was asleep, the snow is coming, she had to leave. Then I glance behind me at Kendall. One nod from her is all it takes.

So I say: "Maybe if you didn't make everything so unpleasant, she wouldn't want to run away."

Big E laughs. Actually opens up his mouth so I can see the gold fillings in his teeth. Goes *ha-ha-ha*.

"What do I make so unpleasant?" he asks.

"Uh . . . everything?"

Shit. That just came out. But Big E laughs again. Definitely not the wrath-of-the-ages reaction I'd imagined.

"You're a kid, Maxie. Only kids use words like *unpleasant*. You have no idea."

Something breaks loose in me now.

"And *you* have no idea! Suze has a life! Don't you see what it's doing to her, trying to take care of you?"

My grandfather stares at me as if he's never actually seen me until this second. I open my mouth again, and this is what spills out:

"Why are you bothering to keep living if you're going to spend all your time being a jerk to everyone? Don't you think Nanny would be heartbroken to see that?"

I can't have uttered that. It's not possible.

Big E doesn't laugh at this, but he does grin. Shows so much of his teeth, the white glows in the half-dark room. He drops his head back, stares at the ceiling. He seems to be traveling miles away.

"If she could see me," he says after a few long moments, "Nanny would be relieved that I haven't changed much."

Something comes over him. Sadness and calm. "I made nothing easy for her. She made nothing easy for me. That's how we worked."

Memories of my grandmother come rushing in. I remember her laugh and the way she loved to tickle-fight. Her glasses sliding down on her nose when she read to me. How her hair looked right after she dyed it, slightly purple in the sun.

Rolling her eyes at Big E. Shaking her head at him as she said, "Wrong again, Mister."

Holy shit. This is what he wants. He wants someone to challenge him at every turn. He needs it and misses it. Without it, he's all alone.

"Okay," I finally say. "You're a jerk. You want us to treat you like one."

Big E takes a deep breath, lowers his head to look right at me. Into me. Like he's seeing me for the first time. "*Exactly.*"

Kendall leans against one of the elevator's wood panels. Sighs. It's been an epic day and she must be as exhausted as I am. Still, I'm a little sad to see her go.

The elevator doors open onto the lobby, and Tony, the night doorman, gives me a look.

"What?" I ask.

"You guys think you're going somewhere?"

"I was going to put my friend in a cab."

He proceeds to laugh his ass off.

I step closer to the door. Oh.

It's white outside. Like, all there is and ever has been, is white. I step closer still, and I can't even see the street.

"Looks like you're staying a while," I tell Kendall.

Before she can respond, her phone starts making a racket. A bunch of texts coming in at once.

"My brother's been trying to reach me," she says, scanning the screen.

"Cell service must be spotty, with the storm."

Kendall walks a few feet away from me and makes a call.

"Hey," she says. "I just got your texts now. I'm okay, I'm at Max's . . . Yes, *him* . . . He says I can stay here . . . I'll call you in the morning . . . No, it's fine, really . . . Emerson, shut up, I said it was fine."

She ends the call and looks sheepishly at me. "He feels guilty about making me wander around the neighborhood in a snowstorm. Maybe I'll get a gift card out of it."

The elevator ride back up is short, but feels long.

I say, "Think of Big E's as a kitschy boutique hotel."

Kendall smiles. "It'll be an upgrade. At Emerson's, I have to sleep in a closet."

Back at the apartment, I show her Aunt Suze's old bedroom and find some fresh sheets. By "fresh," I mean just "clean." The sheets look like they were purchased in 1981. The frolicking rainbow unicorns on them have faded to gray.

"What does your aunt do?" she asks, looking around.

"What do you mean?"

"Like, as a job."

"Oh . . . she used to be in finance. But at the moment, she's a mom."

Kendall nods, as if this information affects how well she'll sleep. We stand there, awkwardly. I'm still holding the sheets because I haven't been able to figure out how to make the bed for her without it feeling ridiculously intimate. Finally, thankfully, she takes them from me.

"There are blankets in that chest," I say, pointing.

Kendall nods again, then drops the sheets on the bed. "Are you tired? Because I'm not."

I'm not either. I may not be tired ever again.

"We could watch a movie," I suggest.

I show her the den, the walls lined with bookshelves and an old TV in one corner. She runs her finger along the spines of all twenty-two volumes of the 1977 World Book Encyclopedia. Then she scans the wall of DVDs and VHS tapes. Yes, we have VHS tapes. Dating back from the dawn of the format. She pulls one off a shelf.

"*Labyrinth?*" she asks. I'm not sure where she's going with this. *Labyrinth* is one of my favorite movies ever. Possibly because I watched this particular videotape every time I visited my grandparents.

"Is that what you want to watch?" I ask, keeping my voice neutral but my guard up.

"Are you kidding?" replies Kendall, totally deadpan. "David Bowie and Muppets? What could possibly be a more awesome way to spend a blizzard?"

I exhale and for the first time, this sensation of *awkward oh shit horrible* is replaced by *fun cool fun*.

Microwave popcorn happens next. We each take a cream soda from Big E's supply in the fridge. "This is the boutique hotel minibar," I tell her. "We replace them before my grandfather notices, then we don't get charged."

As I'm setting up the movie, Kendall goes to the window and draws aside the curtain.

"Whoa," she says. It's really coming down. Wind whips through the alley and rattles the window glass. Kendall presses a single palm to the pane. "So cold."

"Come on," I say, patting the other end of the couch. When she sits, I toss a crocheted blanket at her. She draws it up under her chin.

"I love how everything in this apartment manages to be old, but classy," she says, smelling the blanket.

"It comes automatically with the Park Avenue address."

And my grandmother. She made that blanket. I'm really glad Kendall doesn't say anything snarky about it.

We watch and eat and drink. And make sarcastic but affectionate comments about the movie. Every few minutes, the window shudders against another gust from the blizzard. Whenever I need to shift position on the couch, I'm careful to make sure there's still a few feet between us.

When the movie's over, Kendall heaves a loud, dramatic sigh.

"God, I needed to see that again," she says. "My oldest

brother, Sullivan, introduced me to that movie. It's like, the only thing we have in common."

I turn off the television, and we can hear the wind screeching. It's a high, nefarious sound.

"The snow's going to look really cool tomorrow," I say.

She nods, but looks pained. Bites her lip. "I worry about anyone getting stuck out there."

"You mean, the homeless?" Kendall nods. "I'm pretty sure they're escorted to shelters if they don't go on their own."

"Stuff happens, though. People get missed. Or they think they can stay in their cars. Also, I think about animals. Stray cats. Squirrels."

"I really wouldn't worry about the squirrels. They'll survive the apocalypse."

"Okay. But cats . . ."

"They find places. They know how to survive."

We're quiet for a moment, listening. I can't remember the last time I sat, just listening, to anything.

Then, suddenly, Big E's voice from the other room. "Maxie?"

"Be right back," I tell Kendall.

My grandfather has adjusted his recliner so it's in the most upright position, and he's staring out the window. His blanket has fallen to the floor. There's an infomercial blaring on TV.

"Here," I say, grabbing the blanket and draping it over him.

"The Weather Channel says we were getting over a foot," he says.

"It'll be more than that. There's probably a foot already."

"I hate this snow bullshit," says Big E. "I should be packing for Florida."

"I know," I say, out of instinct. Then I remember. "Wait. No. You said Florida was boring. And you love the snow. You skied until you were seventy-nine!"

Big E looks at me sideways, like it was a secret about himself he didn't want anyone to know.

"Well, I hate it now that I can't ski anymore."

I look at him there in his recliner, his legs small and meek under the blanket. It's hard to imagine he ever skied. Or moved around in the world as a participating member of society.

"What does the weather matter to you?" I ask. "It could be eighty degrees and sunny out there, and you'd still be sitting in this chair watching a commercial for . . . antiaging skin cream."

He looks mad. Then, he smiles. "Point well-taken, Maxie. Well-taken."

"Do you need anything else? I'm going to bed."

"Eh. I'll be asleep again in a minute."

I turn to walk away, then stop, turn back. "Kendall's staying in Aunt Suze's room tonight. She couldn't get home through the storm."

Big E closes his eyes and nods. "That's gentlemanlike. That's good." Then his eyes pop open. "Can she cook us breakfast in the morning?"

"*I'll* cook us breakfast in the morning, you sexist relic."

He smiles. The eyes close again. "Wake me when it's ready."

When I return to the den, Kendall's asleep with the *I*

volume of the encyclopedia spread open on her stomach. I gingerly remove it and place it on a nearby table, but not before noting what page she was on: the entry for Ireland. I wonder if that's one of the places she visited on her trip.

It's been a week-long day, but I'm still wired. I sit down on my end of the couch and grab the remote. Turn the volume down low. Find the same infomercial that was on Big E's TV. I can see the appeal. On infomercials, problems are universal. Solutions are easy.

Everyone's happy in the end.

DECEMBER 30

Max

WHEN I OPEN MY EYES, THERE'S LIGHT COMING through the window. It's not normal morning light. Not sun, exactly, but illumination.

I'm not in a bed. I'm in the den, still. On the couch. My neck stiff and the throw pillow under my face wet with drool.

My feet are tangled up in something.

Another person.

Even though my head and Kendall's head are on opposite sides of the couch, our feet and ankles have clearly made their own arrangements.

I try to withdraw mine, slowly, so I don't wake her up.

This wakes her up.

"Huh!" she yelps.

"It's okay, it's just me," I whisper.

She looks confused, then relieved. Then she glances down at our legs. Now she's confused again.

"Did we both sleep in here?" she asks.

"Yes." Then I add, "Not on purpose," which sounds so incredibly dumb, I wince.

Kendall extracts her ankles from mine. Curls her legs close to her body and wraps the blanket around herself.

"Is it over?"

"What?"

"The blizzard."

"Oh. I think so."

I get up and go to the window, open the curtain. Holy shit, there's a lot of snow out there. Hence the super-neon quality of morning light.

Kendall joins me at the window. Down below on Eighty-Second, the plows have come through, leaving a mountain range of snow piles where sidewalks used to be. Two figures dressed in head-to-toe orange are slowly shoveling the entrance of a building. A person-bundle walks their dog down the middle of the street.

"Let's go outside!" chirps Kendall.

"Now?"

"Why not? This is the best time."

"That's not snow. That's a big F-U from Mother Nature."

"All the more reason to enjoy it."

I grab the remote and try to turn on the TV, but it just clicks. I reach to turn on a lamp. More clicking.

"Power's out," I say. "There's a generator, though. I should go check on . . ."

"Maxie!" comes the bellowing voice from the living room.

"Oh my God," I say as reality dawns on me. "Big E has nothing to watch. Nothing to watch means he has nothing to do, which means end-times for us all."

Kendall rolls her eyes. "Oh, please."

She marches out of the room. Willingly toward Big E. I follow.

"Good morning, Big E!" she says.

"Is the power out?" he asks. He seems to be sitting up straighter. His eyes actually have some energy in them. Maybe this means he's worried. I've never seen him worried. I don't think I could handle it.

"Yes," says Kendall.

"I'm sure the generator will kick in any minute," I say.

Kendall gives me a mischievous look. Then she grabs a stack of magazines off an organized but barely touched mail pile.

"In the meantime," she tells Big E, "here's some super-interesting reading." She places them on his end table, resting his glasses on a *National Geographic* at the top.

He looks at her, amused. Kendall not being a family member does grant her some immunity. Some.

"Sit and read with me while Maxie makes us breakfast," he says to Kendall. "He said he would."

Big E shoots me a grin. It's unnerving. I might have liked him better when he was scaring the crap out of me.

I'm more than happy to flee to the kitchen to pour cereal and orange juice.

Kendall

BIG E FLIPS THE PAGES OF AN ARTICLE WITH VIVID, glossy pictures of forest fires, and also of the people who fight them. They're determined looking and ash covered.

"Tell me," he says, pointing to a photo of a man posing next to a helicopter. "Do you think he cheats on his taxes?"

I lean over for a closer look. "He does seem angry."

"Hmmm," says Big E. "Maybe that's what I'm picking up. This is what a law career will do to you. You never trust anyone."

"Does it matter? If your mountain's in flames, he's there. Honest or not."

Big E nods. "I've known enough FDNY guys in my time.

They have it where it counts."

He gets a faraway look that's not directed at the TV, so he must be thinking. Maybe about the "time" he mentioned, or about the firefighters he's met. There must be a lot of characters in his past. My own grandparents were all gone by the time I was eight, so I never got a chance to mine their memories for interesting stories and people. I know Max would tell me not to waste my efforts on this one, but I can't help it.

"Have you ever been in a fire?" I ask. It's the first Thought Worm to squiggle loose.

"No. Can't say that I have. My mother survived the Triangle Shirtwaist fire, though. When I was a kid, I heard about it so much that it felt like it had happened to me, too."

I look at Big E's legs under the blanket, his feet in socks, looking so useless they might as well be flippers.

"What would you do if there were a fire in this apartment?" I blurt out. "If nobody could help you, would you try to escape?"

Big E looks at me. Confused or amused, I can't tell.

"Or would you just be all, *Okay, I'm old and this is a good way to go*. Then you'd, like, inhale lots of smoke on purpose or drop out the window."

He stares at me for a few more moments, and I'm not sure if I should have kept my mouth shut for once, but he throws his head back and laughs.

"You're priceless!" he says.

"Just very, very curious. Sorry."

"Don't apologize. And don't stop being curious, even when it pisses people off."

"Okay."

"So tell me more about you. What's your situation? You still have time left at school?"

Time left, like a prison sentence. "Yes. Officially."

"What the hell does that mean?"

"I have one last semester. I'm hoping to find a way to do it without actually going back." Suddenly, it's all spilling out. "I spent the last few months in a study abroad program and it was amazing and I kind of want to keep that up somehow and also live here in the city with my brother. Independent study and the GED, that kind of thing."

I gulp a breath. All that sharing was unexpected, but it's happened before. I realize that I hadn't yet spoken my plan aloud. Now it has depth and dimension. It's not just a Thought Worm any longer.

Big E gets a faraway expression on his face.

"You march to your own drummer," he says.

"Sometimes down a dark alley, but yeah."

He laughs. "Still priceless! You remind me of myself when I was young and stupid."

My turn to laugh. "It's not as much fun as it sounds."

"Maybe not now. But in retrospect, it will be."

I start to reply *If you say so* then remember the new Big E rules.

"You're probably full of it, but thanks."

Big E nods as if this was a completely acceptable response, then turns his head toward the blank TV. At that moment, it makes a robotic *I'm awake!* noise and the lights come back on. Now there's a talking CNN anchor on the screen. She instantly sucks up Big E's attention.

I go to the kitchen, where Max is looking at me with big round eyes.

"Did you hear our conversation?" I ask.

He nods. "I've never been able to talk to him like that. About that kind of stuff."

"Well, maybe now you can."

"Maybe. But you . . ."

Max pauses, and the expression on his face is a little bit wonder and a little bit gratitude. He looks straight into me. I'm not sure I like it (but I let him keep looking).

Finally I say, "I should head back to Emerson's."

Max pauses, and we listen to the refrigerator hum. I'm getting the feeling he doesn't want me to go. I'm getting the feeling I don't want me to go. And what will we tell Jamie about me sleeping over? This is all bad.

Then Max says, "We have some snow stuff you can borrow. I'll walk you back."

It's not a question or even a suggestion. Which means I don't have to think/overthink it, it's just pure, unfiltered information I'm supposed to accept.

Max delivers Big E's breakfast to him, then comes back and motions for me to follow, leading us to a closed door at the very end of the long hall. His hand hovers over the doorknob for a moment, curled into the right shape but not touching it yet. Then he grabs and turns quickly. We step inside the room, where there's a huge bed with a carved headboard, flowery sheets, and about seventeen pillows. It looks like the kind of bed you'd find in a fairy tale, untouched and waiting for a lost princess to return.

"My grandparents' room," says Max. "Check this out."

He opens another door to the biggest closet I've ever seen. *This* closet I could sleep in, and maybe even host a party.

The walls are lined with racks of shoes and purses. Sensible pumps and crocodile bags. Coordinated dress suits hang from the rods. Max scans one wall, then another, then finds what he's looking for on a bottom shelf. He grabs and holds them out triumphantly toward me.

Snow boots with a faux fur lining. At least, I hope it's faux.

"This was all your grandmother's?" I ask, taking the boots.

"She had it going on," he says simply, his eyes traveling along the rods of hanging clothes. Finally, he reaches into one spot and pulls out a snowsuit. Like the kind a little kid would wear, but obviously bigger (although not by much). It's hot pink with white stripes down the sleeves.

"Um . . . ," is what I say.

"This should fit you," says Max, pushing it toward me.

"Um . . . ," I repeat.

"What's the problem? Nanny wore this to ski. In Europe! It's like, couture snow gear."

"I'd feel really weird wearing your late grandmother's stuff."

Weird is only the tip of the iceberg.

"Weird is better than freezing and wet. There's two feet of snow out there. I'm going to find something, too."

I take the snowsuit in my other hand and follow Max back into the room. As he rummages in another, similarly cavernous closet on the opposite wall, I look around. Every flat surface is covered with framed family photos.

"When was the last time your grandfather slept in here?" I ask.

"Not sure," says Max from the closet. "Way before my grandmother died. When his back and hips got bad, it hurt him to sleep lying down."

"Like the Elephant Man," I say, then totally regret it, but I hear him chuckle.

When Max emerges, he's holding a navy blue snowsuit. With white stripes down the sleeves. It matches the one I have.

"I've only seen these outfits in photos. They're so much more awesome in person."

"*Awesome* is not the word I'd choose," I say. Max just smiles.

We leave the room and Max carefully closes the door, hermetically resealing the room into its timeless bubble. I go into Aunt Suze's room to change. Half of me still can't believe I'm putting this stuff on, but the other half likes the game of it. It feels like part of Erica's dare.

"Check the dresser for socks," Max calls from somewhere.

Sure enough, there are huge striped knee-high socks in the

dresser. The snowsuit and boots are a little small, but nothing I can't deal with.

I step into the hallway and there's Max. It's really something.

"You look like a cross between a superhero and the world's tallest two-year-old boy," I say.

"And you look like Aspen Barbie."

"Then we're set."

We go downstairs and outside. The first big snow of the season always reminds me of things I've forgotten: that when it dumps nearly two feet in twelve hours, cars are not cars anymore but big ivory shapes in the landscape that look like they've been there since Stonehenge. The trees are dipped in white cake icing. Max takes in the altered city around us and I wonder if he thinks what I think: that it doesn't seem quite real, all quiet and monochromatic like this.

Max steps over the mountain ridge of snow to the street. It's been plowed, but there's still enough snow on the pavement to make driving hazardous, and walking only slightly less so. But the sidewalk, or at least the area where I know the sidewalk should be, is completely impassable. Max offers his hand to help me over the ridge and I take it. As I go, I catch my foot. He steadies me. Then I'm on the other side and upright and really happy I'm wearing these boots and don't even care if it *is* real fur.

We walk one, two, then three and four steps holding hands. Who's supposed to let go first?

On the fifth step, Max lets go of my hand and we begin to trudge up Park. The MetLife Building glows in the distance behind us, lit up even though it's not even eight in the morning. The Christmas trees lining the strip down the center of the avenue are dark, though. So are the traffic lights.

"Power must be out in this whole area," says Max.

A single, brave (or stupid) cab makes its way slowly downtown. At the same time, a snowplow truck is lumbering toward Park from Eighty-Third Street. Max looks at one, then the other, then walks farther into the intersection.

"Watch out!" I yell.

He steps hesitantly at first, then more confidently. When he gets to a spot in the middle of Park, he holds up both hands: one to the cab, one to the plow. Both vehicles slowly come to a halt. Max looks at me.

"The plow first!" I shout. He nods, then motions for the plow to move forward, stepping out of the way to let it pass. The driver actually tips his hat to Max as he goes by. Now the cab continues on its way, but the driver doesn't look at either of us.

We're so busy feeling proud of this traffic control that neither of us sees the other cab.

Max

I TURN TOWARD KENDALL. THE COLD HAS TURNED
her cheeks nearly the color of the snowsuit. She looks *awake*.
And beautiful.

A loud *HONK* from behind me makes me jump. I spin
toward the sound.

The cab's trying to brake but having trouble, fishtailing one
way, then the other. I throw myself into the snowbank at the
curb just as the cab comes to a stop a few feet away.

I see the driver drop his head against the steering wheel,
his back heaving. After a few moments, he raises his head, rolls
down the window. Glares at me.

"You all right, kid?" he barks.

"Yes," I say from my burrow.

"What the hell were you doing in the street?"

"Trying to direct traffic. I didn't see you coming."

The driver shakes his head. "Don't be an idiot."

I bite my lip and nod, surprised to find I'm fighting back tears. The driver mutters under his breath and rolls up the window, then continues on. That could have gone worse. He could have unleashed a string of classic taxi driver curses at me. Or, of course, I could have died.

Kendall stands over me now, offering her hand to help me up.

"Come on," she says.

"I don't want to count all that," I say. "Because that was stupid."

She looks like she wants to protest, but then searches my face. Does she see how I almost cried? Does she see I have no idea why I almost cried?

Good stuff cancels out bad stuff, bad stuff cancels out good stuff. It's never ending. What's the point?

But here's Kendall, pulling me to standing. She lets go of my hand and brushes the snow off my back. She gets me ready to continue on.

A few blocks farther up Park, there's a man and a woman outside an apartment building, working hard to clear the sidewalk. He's trying to push a snowblower while she shovels. Underneath the building's front awning, there's a stroller covered in plastic. Inside, a baby wrapped up like a burrito is screaming bloody murder.

"Good morning," I say.

The woman stops and leans on her shovel, panting. "Yeah. Good morning." She doesn't look like she agrees.

"Do you need help?" asks Kendall.

"No, thanks," says the woman, while at the same time the man asks, "What kind of help?"

"Just . . . help," I say. "With whatever."

The couple exchange a look. "Would we get in trouble?" he asks her.

"So what if we did?" replies the woman. Then she turns to me. "It's the snowblower. Hard to push when it's this deep."

Kendall moves to the stroller and peeks in, then motions to the woman. Points to the baby, then to herself. The woman nods. Kendall lifts the plastic barrier and picks up the baby, who's now reached the point where its cries don't sound human anymore. Kendall looks a little scared, but she holds the baby close and starts bouncing it up and down. Making a loud *Shhhhhhhh* noise. The baby's cries slow down and fade a little. It's like turning the volume knob to the left.

"She likes that," says the woman to Kendall. "Thank you."

I step up to the snowblower and the man backs away, clearly glad to be putting some distance between himself and this machine. He puts one hand to his chest. Checks out my snowsuit, then glances at Kendall. I'm sure he has questions.

I give the snowblower a push. It inches through the snow,

but not easily. Clearly not meant for this kind of load. But this is where being tall comes in handy, because I can really get some leverage on it. I push again, an unplanned *oof* sound coming out of me, and gain some momentum. The snow spurting out of the blower is my own personal blizzard. Maybe this is what a god feels like, making weather.

Over by the door, Kendall is showing the baby the arc of blasting snow. She points, whispers in its ear. It's only whimpering now. The woman smiles at them and keeps shoveling.

Ten minutes later, the walkway is clear. Or at least, clear enough. Kendall hands the baby to its mother. The man comes over to me and turns off the snowblower.

"I can't thank you enough," he says.

"It was no problem."

"You're a good person," he adds, then slips something into the pocket of my snowsuit.

I shake my head, push my hand in the pocket to give him back whatever he just gave me.

"Please," he says, gripping my arm and holding it in place.

There's a pleading quality to his expression. It's important to him. Finally, I nod.

Kendall comes over. Her smile plus the rosy cheeks equals completely lovely.

"Our work is done here," she says, pretending to wipe her hands clean. "Tune in tomorrow, boys and girls, for another episode of the Ski Bunny Squad!"

I laugh. We wave to the husband and wife as we make our

way down the street. The baby looks unconvinced.

"Can we count that as two?" asks Kendall.

"Don't think so."

"Fine. I'll write it all down later. But for the record, that was a big one. You pushed a big heavy thing and exerted yourself, and I braved a banshee child."

I reach into the pocket of the jacket and pull out a ten-dollar bill. Hold it out to her.

"What's that?" she asks.

"The guy. He gave it to me. Or I should say, he forced me to accept it."

She stares at the money. "I'm conflicted."

"Are you?"

"On the one hand, that's ten bucks! We could go get some overpriced hot chocolate as soon as a café opens up."

"And on the other hand?"

"It changes the way I feel about what we did."

"I know," I say, staring at the money. "We made that rule about money for a reason."

"But that's not why we stopped," she says. "That wasn't our intention. I think we should focus on that." We walk in silence for a few moments. When we reach the corner of the next block, Kendall stops and says, "I have an idea." She holds out her hand. "Give me the money."

She smiles wickedly as I hand her the bill. For a second, I think she's going to pocket it and run off down the street.

Instead, she rolls it into a tight little tube, walks over to the nearest mound of snow. Shoves her arm in up to the shoulder. When she pulls it out, the money's gone.

"Someone will find it tomorrow after a little of the snow melts. It'll make their day."

"You know we can't count that as a kindness. We agreed."

"This one's just for fun," she says, her eyes dancing again.

"And I thought you wanted to get hot chocolate."

"At my brother's apartment, they have completely ridiculous hot chocolate for free."

She grins at me and I grin back, like we've claimed something together. This whole frosted city, or the block we're standing on. Or maybe, simply, this moment. One moment, when there is nobody else on earth I'd rather be with.

"Onward," says Kendall. We continue walking.

I look back to where she stuck the money and hope whoever finds it isn't an asshole.

Ulysses

IT'LL BE PERFECT, TALLY PROMISED ME.

Her uncle's building on the Upper East Side needed a
superintendent. The job came with a basement apartment and
a grab bag of other perks.

We needed a place to live that wasn't my parents' house in
Queens.

We needed something different.

We needed something.

We needed.

I'm really tired of needing.

The baby's sick. Not in a cancer way, where you can put
up a page online for people to send you money because they

feel bad for you. She's just sick. Always sick. A cold, an ear infection, something called croup that, no joke, makes your kid sound like a barking seal. There's nothing officially wrong with her. She has a shitty immune system, and nobody's going to send you money through the internet for that.

Tally's so focused on the baby, she doesn't need extra stress. So I don't tell her about my chest pains. About how sometimes I can't take a breath deep enough to fill me up.

I used to be a firefighter. Breathing bad stuff that hangs out forever in your lungs is part of the job.

There's also something called stress. My friend Alex had that. He thought he was dying, and at the emergency room, they told him it was just a panic attack. He felt like a giant moron.

I don't want to feel like that. But every time I go to sleep, I'm not sure I'm going to wake up.

These kids who stopped to help us. They're so clueless. I would give anything to be that clueless again. That tall boy's got nothing to worry about except a cute girl to hang with. He didn't need my money, but I needed to give it to him. I needed to not need, and ten bucks seemed to be the price of that.

When I was that kid's age, I thought I would get everything I wanted. I thought that even if today wasn't perfect, tomorrow would be. Because I deserved it. I deserved everything and when you deserve something, it just comes. God, I wish I could go back in time and kick myself in the ass.

You have to take life by the hand, even though you never

know where it's going to drag you. You don't always have control. But what's the option? Letting go?

It's possible to have no regrets but also wish everything were different.

Kendall

WE REACH THE CORNER OF NINETY-SIXTH STREET
and this is where we should turn right, toward Emerson's.

I'm not ready for this to end, so I look to the left and two long blocks down, I can see the park.

"Let's go that way," I say, pointing left.

"I thought we were going to Emerson's," says Max.

"We need to go there first," I point again, jabbing at the air with my finger, hoping Max will get the hint so I don't have to say it.

"The park?" he asks.

"I've never seen it buried in fresh snow."

He considers that. "Me neither. Okay, let's do it."

We cross and start walking toward Madison, right down the middle of the street. More people are coming out now. Mostly building personnel, shoveling and snowblowing, and folks with dogs. There are a few families, carrying sleds or dragging them behind, and even the kids' snow gear looks less dorky than ours. We follow the trickle of people to the nearest park entrance.

And wow. The paths aren't even plowed yet, so everyone's just diving into the vast ocean of white, and they really do look like they're swimming in something. One kid runs up the nearest hill, then rolls down, squealing in a way you can't squeal in normal life.

We're laughing and pointing, and I feel good about the world, and I think maybe Max does too. This is when out of nowhere, for no obvious reason, he takes my hand.

A second passes. I don't breathe.

"Oh my God!" he bursts out, letting go and backing up. "Sorry! For a second I thought . . ."

"I was Eliza?"

"A reflex, I guess. What the hell is wrong with me?"

"Don't worry about it," I say, although actually I think he should worry about it.

"Sometimes my brain hates me."

"Oh, well then, you know what I feel like pretty much all the time."

Max simply frowns. I get it. He's embarrassed, I'm weirded out, and it's not an easy-fix situation. Usually this is where anxiety turns me into one giant, redheaded impulse. Which might explain why this comes out of my mouth next:

"We're not going to deal with what happened last summer, are we?"

Max looks at me for a few long seconds, like maybe he's trying to find a way to avoid answering. Finally, he goes over to a nearby bench, bends down and sweeps an armful of snow away from it, and sits in the space he made. I walk over and stand in front of him.

"What do you mean, *deal with it?*" he asks, raising his eyes to me.

"Bring it up. Get it out in the open."

Max sighs. "Open is good, I guess." He pauses, scoops up some snow in his mittened hand and forms it into a ball. "So what would you like me to do?"

"Can we just acknowledge that it happened?"

"Okay. It happened."

"I'm sorry," I say, and it's really just a reflex, like blurting out *Excuse me* when you bump someone.

"I'm not," says Max.

I clear my own bench space, sit down, and turn to face him. He turns to face me and the air between us takes a different shape and maybe even a different color. Like before it was blue, and now it's turning turquoise. We can have this conversation because the world is not real right now. It's a temporary, snow-covered one that's disappearing by the minute.

Max says, "See, Eliza and I worked things out after that

209

night, but only for a little while. It was the beginning of the end for us, really. An end that was a hundred percent going to happen anyway. Without that stuff between you and me, it would have dragged on longer."

"So, there was a silver lining."

He smiles at me. "I guess so. Was there a silver lining for you, too?"

I have to think about this. He doesn't know that he was my first kiss. He doesn't know that in those minutes when we were sitting there and I was crying and he was listening, I felt something unexpected: excitement that finally *finally* something interesting was happening to me. I had the same kind of drama in my life that everyone else seemed to have.

When he leaned forward and kissed me on the cheek, I was the one who turned my head.

"There was," I say, simply.

Now I look at Max's face, which is no longer the same face it was back then because of everything we've shared in the last few days. I'm so grateful for all of it, and for him.

"Feel better now?" he asks. "Have we dealt with it?"

"Yes. Thank you."

He smiles. "No problem."

Then he spreads his arms and leans down, offering a hug. I take it, and give him one back. We still don't line up. My cheek is against his neck and his nose is in my hair. Still, we stay that way for a moment and I can't imagine what we look like, in our matching snowsuits. Someone's probably walking by thinking,

That's so cute I want to vomit.

We're not a couple, I mentally say to the theoretical person thinking bad things about us.

But you like him, says a Thought Worm, flailing on the ground in my mind. *You LIKE him like him!*

Screw that, Thought Worm. You're wrong. Okay, sure, I want to kiss him. I want to turn my head and start making out with him right on this freezing bench even though I can't feel my butt anymore. Besides, Jamie Jamie Jamie. I still like Jamie, too.

I wait for Max to break the hug but he doesn't break the hug.

Is this going to become complicated?

God, I hope so, says the Thought Worm.

Suddenly, something's buzzing. Max drops away from me, pulls out his phone, and frowns at the number.

"Hello?" he answers tentatively. "Oh! Hey, Tony. What's up?"

Silence. Max's frown returns and deepens. I can see where he's going to get a really prominent wrinkle when he's older, and also how that wrinkle will just make him even hotter.

"What?" he barks. "How did that happen? Okay, yes. I'm over in the park. I'll get there as fast as I can."

He hangs up and stares at his phone.

"What's the matter?" I ask.

"The generator stopped working. Big E was coming downstairs to get help when it happened, so he got stuck in the elevator."

"Oh my God. Is he okay?"

"Yes, but he's still in there. They're working on it now."

Max puts the phone in his pocket and drops his head into his hands. "Holy shit, I feel awful."

"He told us to go out! The power was on. He said he'd call if he needed anything."

Max shakes his head. "My dad and my aunt are going to kill me. If Big E doesn't do it first."

"Please don't be so hard on yourself. You've been doing everything you were supposed to. Sometimes the unexpected happens."

He stands up, starts sloshing back toward Fifth Avenue as fast as he can. I follow.

"Max!" I call after him. "You had no way of knowing, and also guess what? He's fine! He's in a fancy apartment building full of people. You don't even have the skills to get him out of an elevator."

"But if I'd been there, he wouldn't have been in the elevator to begin with."

I can't argue with that.

Max mutters again. "He must have needed something and it must have been urgent."

He's taking huge strides with his long legs and I'm practically running to keep up.

"Max!" I call again, breathless.

He pauses to wait for me.

"I'm sorry," he says. "I've got to rush over there. Are you

okay to get home by yourself?"

I pant for a moment, then realize what's happening. I'm being ditched.

"Sure."

"Okay . . ." He starts to walk, then stops again, turns back to me. "I'll call you later!"

Then he breaks into a run.

I slowly make my way toward Emerson's, watching the city writhe back to life. The power must be on again, because the traffic lights work and things glow—electric signs and windows and holiday decorations. Everything looks and feels disoriented, or maybe that's me.

I tell myself, I'm glad Max took off. (We'll ignore the fact that he *literally* ran away from me, possibly using the situation with his grandfather to exit a mistake situation.) Forget about the game. We did what we could and maybe that was enough to restore balance to the universe. *I can't see him anymore.* I say it over and over again as I walk, the rhythm of it driving my footsteps in Nanny's boots. Then I switch to a new rhythm: *Jamie Jamie Jamie.*

When I reach Emerson's place, he and Andrew cruelly make me pose for a photo in my snowsuit before I can peel it off and take a hot shower.

I emerge from the Groset in my pajamas. Emerson and Andrew exchange a look, then Andrew disappears into the bedroom.

"Come sit with me in the kitchen," says Emerson. "I'll make you a mocha."

Uh-oh. That can't be good. But I do what I'm told.

After I sit down at their tiny table, my brother sighs. "This is hard for me. I love you, Ken. You're my favorite sister."

"L-O-L."

"*And* sibling. *And* nuclear family member."

"Emerson, you know it was an accident, telling Andrew about the text."

Emerson shrugs. "Accidents still cause damage."

"So what happens now?" I ask.

Emerson glances at the open bedroom door. Takes a sip of his mocha. "I'm going to move out after New Year's."

I bang my hands hard on the table, and even the mammoth mugs aren't big enough to keep mocha from sloshing out.

"You *can't*! Not you guys."

Emerson clucks his tongue in frustration. "I know you need us to be together as a shining example of a healthy relationship, but Andrew and I need something else. We need to know this is what we want, and we won't know that until we spend a little time apart. Neither of us has ever been alone since we came out."

I can't shake the absurd feeling that I'm twelve and my parents just told me they're getting divorced. I push the mocha away, even though it really is the most delicious thing I've ever tasted.

"Where are you going to live?" I ask him.

"Our friend Taj needs a roommate. His parents are loaded and they set him up in a loft downtown in the Meatpacking District. It'll be a shorter commute to school for me."

My bigger question is, how do I fit into all this? If I want to stay in the city, who has room for me? But I know better than to ask right now.

"What about the cat?" I ask instead.

"Louis stays here," says Andrew from the bedroom doorway. "And Emerson will come over a lot to spend time with him *and* me."

I look carefully at Andrew. He appears much, much sadder about this than my brother. My stupid, restless brother.

"You can help me start packing tomorrow," jokes Emerson, but when I give him a dirty look, he adds, "Or not."

"And today, we have a *Twilight* movie marathon," says Andrew. "I'll get some Chinese food and candy bars."

I really hate these guys. They make the saddest breakup ever look absolutely darling.

DECEMBER 31

Max

AUNT SUZE'S VOICE DOWN THE HALL, LOUD AND
forced-energetic.

I've been awake for a while. I just don't want to get out of
bed. Freddie Mercury stares down at me, and his look is disap-
proving today. He has no tolerance for aimlessness. Frankly, I
can't blame him.

Yesterday. Everything about yesterday, running on a loop
in my head.

Big E needed help with the remote control. That's why he
was in the elevator when the generator failed.

Apparently, he sat on one of the seventeen buttons that

nobody ever uses. The TV went to static, and he couldn't figure out how to get back to what he was watching. He tried to call me, but couldn't get through.

Under different circumstances, I'd be laughing my ass off at the thought of my grandfather hauling himself out of the La-Z-Boy. Shuffling into the hallway and into the elevator, remote in hand. My father and aunt and at least three different home aides have tried unsuccessfully to get the guy to take a walk downstairs once a day. Now we know: all they ever had to do was screw with the remote.

But I don't feel like laughing. I'm not used to letting people down. I've never *not* been there when someone needed me.

It feels fucking awful.

You know what else feels awful? Kendall's voice. It's the voice I hear in my head when I'm trying to be okay with this. She'd said, *You've been doing everything you're supposed to.* And intellectually, I know she's right. The power was on when I left. I wasn't going far, and I had my cell phone if Big E needed me. I had no way of knowing that post-blizzard phone service would still be messed up. Or that the generator would implode. Or that my grandfather would actually try to leave the apartment by himself for the first time in an eon.

Something took place, out there in the snow with Kendall. It felt like the first honest day I've had in a long time.

Then I was a douche bag. Ditched her in the middle of a snowbank in Central Park. Plus, her suede boots and wool coat are still by the front door. Oh, and maybe I should have mentioned this right away, but Big E is fine. It takes a lot more than getting stuck in an elevator to dent *that* guy.

My phone starts buzzing.

Several messages from yesterday have finally come through. One from my mom, one from Jamie. One from Eliza.

Hope you weathered the storm. You never answered me about New Year's, asshole.

I hadn't even thought about New Year's. Jamie's coming into the city, but to be with Kendall.

I don't want to be alone. I don't want her to be with him and for me to be with nobody.

Hey, I type back to Eliza. **Just got your message now. Storm was cool.**

I pause, my thumbs hovering. Quivering, even. Eh, what the hell.

Come to the city tonight.

It feels like a low-risk proposition. She probably made other plans five minutes after she texted me.

Yes, comes her message back.

A flooding swirl of relief.

You can stay in a spare bedroom here, I write. Look at me, laying down parameters. Setting boundaries.

Suddenly, there's knocking.

"Max? Max, it's Suze. Are you up?"

"Yes!"

"Are you decent? I'm coming in."

She doesn't wait for my reply and opens the door. It's fine,

I slept in my clothes. My aunt looks more tired than I've ever seen her.

"Let's say a little prayer, shall we?" says Suze.

"For what?"

"This new aide. Katherine. She'll be here any minute."

The aide! Holy freedom, thank God for the aide.

"So you're hereby relieved of your duties, Max. I can't thank you enough for what you've done."

Maybe she doesn't know about yesterday.

"And don't worry about yesterday," she adds.

"Is it okay if I stay until tomorrow?" I ask. "I have a friend coming in for New Year's. She'd like to crash in your old bedroom."

Suze laughs. "Of course. Man, I wish I could be in the city tonight. New Year's Eve . . . I could tell you some stories."

She gets a faraway look in her eyes. Then the doorman buzzes up.

"Showtime," says Suze.

She disappears and a minute later, I hear her welcoming someone into the apartment.

When I finally get out of bed, make myself presentable, and emerge from the bedroom, I find Suze and the new aide standing on either side of Big E.

The aide turns when I walk into the room. "Hi," she says, her voice rough and gravelly. "I'm Katherine."

I shake her hand. She looks like she's been around. She looks like she could beat me up if necessary.

"Your grandfather was just telling me how much he enjoyed spending time with you," she says matter-of-factly.

"I don't think he enjoys spending time with anyone," I reply. "You know he's the biggest curmudgeon on the Upper East Side."

"Max!" says Suze, alarmed. She shoots an apologetic look at Big E.

But Big E laughs. "He's right, of course," he says. "Although I hate it less with him than most people."

"Hopefully you'll feel the same way about me," says Katherine, but Big E makes a growl-sigh hybrid sound.

I beckon her and Suze into the kitchen.

"Listen," I whisper as we huddle together. "I want you to try something."

Then I tell them. That Ezra Levine does not want us to be respectful or considerate or polite. He does not want things to go unsaid. That the uglier the truth, the louder he needs us to shout it. That he wants us to challenge and argue and call things as they are. That it was Nanny's way, and Nanny's way is forever.

Suze looks unconvinced, but Katherine grins. I can tell right away that she gets it. "Honey," she says, "if all that's true, I was *made* for this job."

So I figured out this thing about my grandfather. Figured it out *for* him. For all of us, really. That kindness doesn't always look or sound like kindness; sometimes it comes in disguise. Actually, it was Kendall who decoded that puzzle.

Kendall.

I'm so sure, suddenly, of how much I want to be with her. Not just right now but every day, for a long, long time. As much as humanly possible. In other words, I'm in deep shit.

"Maxie!" booms Big E. "Come here a second!"

As always, I go where I'm summoned. In the living room, my grandfather's shuffling through the drawer in his end table.

"What's up?" I ask.

"I forgot, I have something to give you. An idea I had." He finally finds what he's searching for. Holds up a sealed white business envelope. "Don't open it now. Just . . . take a look when you get a free moment."

He hands off the envelope casually, like he's asking me to put it in the recycling bin. It's light. I know what it must be: another magazine article he thinks I should read. I fold the envelope in half and tuck it into a back jeans pocket. Unless it's a detailed guide on how to tell a girl you might be in love with her even though she's beginning to date one of your best friends, it's the last fucking thing I need right now.

I'm walking up Park Avenue with a shopping bag filled with Kendall's boots and coat when I realize I don't have her brother's address. I start to text her, but find myself calling instead.

"Max," says Kendall. I can't read anything into her voice. She's simply making a statement out of my name.

"Hey, Kendall." I can play this game, too. Although, yeah. I'm the one who called her. So that's stupid.

"How's your grandfather?" she asks.

"He's fine. The new aide starts today."

There's a pause.

"Jamie's coming in later," says Kendall. Her words hang straight and flat, like on a clothesline.

"Oh, right," I say, as if I just remembered this and wasn't thinking about it all morning. I'm about to tell her about Eliza, but then have a moment of intelligence. "So I want to get your stuff back to you, but I don't know where your brother lives."

She gives me the address, then adds, "If nobody's here, buzz the neighbor in 3C. She'll hang on to it for me."

We hang up. I don't say any of the things that might make New Year's Eve go differently for both of us. I don't make a grand gesture. I'm a whimper, not a bang.

So, that's it. She'll be with Jamie tonight and I'll be with Eliza. Whatever that ends up meaning.

Then tomorrow, back home. Back to the call center and my parents' house and Limbo Unlimited.

If someone told me a few days ago that I'd be sad to leave Big E's apartment, I would have laughed my ass off.

Ezra Levine

THEY SAY, YOUR BODY IS A TEMPLE.

That's bullshit. My body is like Madison Square Garden: huge and filled with strange happenings. Rock bands I've never heard of. Sports teams I don't care about. Screaming and yelling and thumping I can't control.

It's not entirely my fault that my body is like this. I don't have genetics on my side.

But yeah, I did let it get this way. I stopped caring. Maureen cared enough for both of us, even when she didn't want to. Even when she thought I was being a royal jackass, she couldn't help caring. When she died, I took whatever replacement people offered.

Max asked me why I want to keep living. And that's a damn good question.

At first I thought it was just stubbornness. Not wanting to do what someone expects me to do, which in this case is to go ahead and drop dead. Then I figured, maybe not stubbornness but laziness. I'm living because that's what happens if I do nothing. I keep breathing. I keep waking up after I fall asleep. Living is simply the status quo and I don't have the energy to change it.

I thought that until Max's friend asked me what I'd do if the building were on fire. If I'd try to get out, or let the smoke consume me. Or perhaps jump from a window to certain death. I keep turning that over in my head. The truth is that if and when the fire comes, I'm running for my goddamn life.

Running. Walking. Crawling. Whatever the hell I can manage.

For my life. Such that it is.

I've known a lot of pain, and not only the physical kind. I've caused a lot of pain, too. That's the stuff I'll be glad to leave behind when I finally make my exit.

I just hope I'm allowed to take the good stuff with me. There's more of it than I ever thought.

Max. I wonder when he's going to open that envelope.

I wonder if he's going to do the right thing with what's inside.

Kendall

I'M SITTING ON THE BED IN MY GROSET, WATCHING
Emerson pull clothing off hangers and drop them into a
moving box. He can start moving into his new place today,
apparently—just in time for a New Year's Eve party there. I'm
planning to bring Jamie. Andrew's gone out because he doesn't
want to witness The Packing.

"How can you tell whose clothes are whose?" I ask him. "I
mean, you guys must wear the same size."

"You recognize your own clothes, don't you?"

"Yeah, but guy clothes are all pretty much the same."

Emerson gives me a dirty look. "I'm going to pretend you
never said that."

I know he's trying to stay in a good mood, play the role of the one who wanted to leave. But I can tell by the curl of his lower lip that this is still really shitty for him.

The buzzer rings from downstairs. Emerson moves to the intercom, but I grab his arm.

"It's Max, dropping off my stuff."

"Okay."

"I want him to leave it with Bonnie."

"O-kay," says Emerson.

"It's just easier if I don't see him right now."

"Easier," he presses.

"Oh my God, I'll explain later."

The buzzer goes off again, and Emerson raises one eyebrow at me, positively tantalized. I find myself holding my breath, as if Max could hear me breathe from all the way downstairs.

Emerson shakes his head. There's a long pause.

"Pathetic," he says. Instinctively, I shush him.

But there's no more buzzing after that. Ten minutes later, after I hear Bonnie go downstairs, then come back up, I go over to get the bag.

"I can't thank you enough," I tell her.

She shakes her head and laughs. "Sweetheart, I have been in your place so many times, I keep a toothbrush there."

When I step outside, wearing my Paris flea market dress again, it hits me. I'm going to meet Jamie at Grand Central and we'll let the hours unroll from there. This is happening.

I keep wanting to think about Max but every time, I can stop that thinking by bringing up the image of Jamie and our painfully quick pre-kiss outside the deli. Maybe spending time with him again will send me back to that moment, before Luna, before the Bystanding, before Max and our dare. Maybe I'll be able to move on from that street corner.

It's strange to be out here, navigating the post-storm snow in my thin boots and wool coat, no longer hermetically sealed in that snowsuit. There's also something in the air, a promise that tonight everyone's going to have some kind of adventure. Because why wouldn't they? This is New York City on December 31. Who wouldn't want to be here, and how lucky am I to finally be part of it?

My phone dings with a text and I pause to check it. The message is simply a photo of the Hudson River from a train window.

Jamie is actually, truly on his way.

Everything is on its way.

The subway's more crowded than usual and people are acting a little stupid but I don't really blame them. I'd be acting stupid, too, if I had someone to do it with.

The train slows as it approaches the Seventy-Seventh Street station.

The doors open, and almost nobody gets out because this is the kind of day when everyone's getting on, on, on.

Just before the doors close again, I look up to see Max stepping into the car.

He spots me before I can do anything. (And what would I do, really? Throw my coat over my head? Use the old lady next to me as a human shield?) There's a moment when he's not sure where to go, and the train starts moving again. He lurches in my direction, grabbing the pole across from me.

"Fancy meeting you here," he says with a nervous laugh, then pauses, looks me over. "You got your stuff from the neighbor. Good."

"Thanks for dropping it off. Sorry I missed you. I'll get the snowsuit back to you soon." I'm a Liar Liar Pants on Fire, and trying my best not to meet his eyes and definitely not to hear that one little Thought Worm squealing *You like him!* over and over in my head.

"Where are you and Jamie meeting up?" he asks casually.

"At Grand Central."

Max's mouth flattens and then his whole face follows suit, all straight lines and pale.

"What's the matter?" I ask.

"I'm meeting someone at Grand Central, too." He gives me a look.

My heart drops two stories.

"Eliza?"

Max nods. "We're just hanging out as friends."

I believe him, I think, but I can't help being disappointed in him, too. This is getting way too complicated. *Jamie Jamie Jamie.*

We stare at each other as the train rumbles on, jolting us to the right, then the left. Max's huge hand grips the pole tighter and now he leans his head against it, even though that's really unsanitary. Our time together over the past few days, that's like the subway track behind us. Gone and done, and now all that's left is what lies on the other side of this tunnel.

"Eliza and Jamie are riding in together, of course," Max finally says. "She wouldn't want to travel alone."

"Even though she knows Jamie's coming in to meet me?"

"It's been a few months. She probably figures, if she sees you, she can handle it."

"What about me? What if I don't want to see her?" Panic rises up in my throat at the thought of her face in front of mine. I pull out my phone. "I should text Jamie and ask him to meet me somewhere else. Away from her."

I start typing, my fingers missing half the keys.

"Kendall," says Max, reaching down and taking my phone out of my hand. "What's the big deal, if you see her?"

I look up at him. He's asking a real question; his eyes are round and dark with concern and curiosity. So I stare out the train window and pretend that instead of seeing darkness, I see what happens when I face Eliza again for the first time since the night I made out with her boyfriend.

"I guess I can handle it," I say with a sigh. "At least we'll be in a big crowded place crawling with security."

Max rolls his eyes, but doesn't tell me I'm overreacting.

We're silent the rest of the ride.

✳ ✳ ✳

They're supposed to be waiting for us at the information booth in the middle of Grand Central, below the big four-sided clock that seems extra symbolic here on New Year's Eve. Why can't I shake the feeling that time is running out for something?

It's insanely crowded, worse than it was on Fifth Avenue the other day, but I see them as soon as we round the corner into the main terminal: Jamie, taking photos of the star-sprinkled ceiling, and Eliza, leaning against the booth, eyes closed.

"Nobody expects anyone to stick together," whisper-shouts Max. "We'll do our own thing, you guys do yours."

I nod, and of course, *of course*, this is the moment—when Max is leaning forward with his lips at my ear—Eliza spots us. She doesn't seem to react, except to elbow Jamie, who puts down his camera and smiles when he sees me.

Here he comes now. After all the thinking I've been doing about him over the last few days, I'm so glad to see him and have proof that yes, he really does exist.

"Hey, you," he says, and wraps his arms around me and doesn't pull away.

"I'm so glad you're here," I tell him, then look over at Max and Eliza. He stoops to hug her and they kiss each other on the cheek. She doesn't glance at me.

"Don't be mad," says Jamie.

"I ran into Max on the train, so I had advance notice. And it's okay."

Jamie glances back. "You mean, Eliza."

"Yes."

"Okay, so don't be mad I didn't tell you . . ."

"About what?"

But the *what* steps out from the other side of the kiosk.

Ari Logan, aka my best friend, who I haven't seen since I left for Europe last August.

"Oh my God!" I gasp, and within seconds, I'm falling toward her. She's falling toward me. We're hugging tight, tight, tight. Ari's shoulders are still square and solid, and she smells the same, and I'm starting to cry because it's only now that I realize how much I've missed her.

"I know we were going to hang out after Christmas," I begin to say. "I'm sorry I left town again so quickly."

"No worries," she says, then pulls back to examine me. "You look great. Globe-trotting becomes you."

I laugh. "Thanks."

Ari spots something in the distance and smiles. I turn to see.

It's her boyfriend, Camden, winding toward us through the crowd with a Zaro's Family Bakery bag clutched to his chest.

"Hey, thanks for waiting," he says when he reaches us, slipping his non-Zaro's arm around Ari. "I've been thinking about this coffee cake for the last ninety minutes."

"We don't want to cramp your style tonight," says Ari, glancing sideways at Jamie. "But I really wanted to see you before school started again. And it's New Year's Eve, in New York City. We can split up whenever. Camden and I will find things to do."

"No," I say. "There's a party at Emerson's brand-new apartment and I want you guys to come."

Eliza and Max have been chatting, and now Max steps into our circle. "I think we should get out of this crush of people and find somewhere to eat," he says. "Eliza says there's a great noodle house close by."

I glance at Eliza, who looks away. So it's going to be like this, and actually I'm relieved.

We make our way out of Grand Central, walking in formation. Two by two by two. Do we look like dorky kids from upstate clogging Manhattan on New Year's Eve? God, I hope so.

Eventually we make it out the side exit to Lexington Avenue and start walking downtown. Eliza leads the way and it's as if she's always led the way; how did we ever get around the city without her leading the way? When we pass a young couple begging on one corner, Max turns to look back at me. We haven't talked about the dare because I assumed we were done, but we have three kindnesses left, points to score, spaces to fill. A flicker in Max's expression says, *We're still on.*

Ari and Camden walk ahead of Jamie and me, holding hands, which feels extra awkward for us. It's like a message from my near future. *IF YOU DON'T SCREW THIS UP, YOU'LL BE HOLDING HANDS TOO!* After we stop at a light and then start moving again, I make sure Jamie and I are in front of them.

Eliza steers us to the door of a restaurant and we pour inside. The place is tiny so the staff scrambles to push together three tables where we can all fit. I sit down in the chair on the end, Jamie sits across from me, and Ari next to me. Eliza moves to the other side of Ari, and now she and I can't really see each other.

This is ridiculous. At some point we're going to have to speak and acknowledge the other's existence and possibly even interact. And why isn't Max noticing this and doing something about it? It makes so much sense to blame this on Max.

Once I let myself be mad at him, I realize how awesome it feels to be mad at him. It feels a little like freedom. Why didn't I think of this before?

Max

THERE'S SOMETHING WRONG.

Eliza's happy.

Her smiles come too quickly. They last too long.

She's simply not Eliza. She's a version that would be much easier to share the world with, but easily sharing the world is not really the point of someone like her. And I mean that in the best possible way. Really.

What's up with you? I write on the back of a napkin. Slide it across the table to her as she expertly maneuvers her chopsticks through a bowl of udon noodles and broth.

She reads it, snorts a laugh. Wipes her mouth with the napkin.

"Max, everything's fine. Don't be such a helicopter parent."
She goes back to her food. Camden leans into my ear.

"You're noticing this too?" he asks. I nod. "I have some theories," he continues. "We'll talk later."

Across the table, Ari watches Camden. There's so much tenderness in her half grin, I'm overcome with jealousy. When Camden left our school to go to Ari's, I thought it was a mistake. What could be more cliché than following a girl somewhere? Then I figured it out: I felt this way because I was doing the exact same thing. Putting off school so I could be around for Eliza. I was following her by staying in place.

My choice had been the wrong one. Clearly, Camden's wasn't.

I peer down to the other end of the table, where Jamie and Kendall are chatting, their heads close. He's gesturing with a soup spoon, waving it around, drawing pictures in the air.

I excuse myself to the restroom. When I'm done and open the door, Camden's waiting outside. Without thinking, I pull him into the bathroom with me.

"Dude," he says, laughing. "This is not that kind of place."

I'm dying to hear Camden's theories about Eliza, but those will have to wait. I've got a more pressing question. "How exactly did all this happen?" I ask. "Did Jamie invite you and Ari to come with him tonight?"

"Yes. Why do you seem surprised?"

"It sounded like he and Kendall had planned some epic romantic evening together."

"I think they did, but now he's a little freaked out."

"About what?"

Camden shrugs. "How much he likes her."

"Oh, for fuck's sake," I say. "I won't let him break Kendall's heart again." As soon as these words come out of my mouth, I realize how strongly I feel them. "He's got to man up."

Camden nods. "Totally agree."

"Then promise me this," I say. "Make sure Kendall has the kind of night she wants. And expects. And deserves."

Camden frowns. "How do you know what kind of night she expects?"

I pause. *The truth, Max.* "We've hung out a bit in the last couple days."

"What?"

"You can't tell Eliza."

Camden smiles. "There must be a good story behind this."

I shrug to say *sure yeah it is* but really, it's more than a good story. It's more than any story. How can I describe the last few days since Luna? Describing it feels like giving it away.

I'm going to keep it.

Lunch is fun. We eat, we slurp. I watch Eliza carefully, trying to figure out what's up. She won't look at Kendall, but frankly I'd be more worried if she did.

"So," I say after we split up the check. "What happens now?"

"Kendall and I want to head downtown until her brother's

party," says Jamie. "Walk around Greenwich Village, SoHo, get some photos."

"And we're tagging along," adds Camden.

"Count me out," says Eliza. "One of my cosplay friends is playing in a band at a bar in Chelsea, so Max and I will make our way over there."

"We will?" I ask her.

"Oh, yes."

"Which friend?"

"Captain America." I know Captain America. Who happens to be a girl.

"But that's not until later, I'm sure," I tell Eliza. "Why don't we hang out with these guys until then?"

I'd like to watch how Jamie is with Kendall. Holy shit, I *am* a helicopter parent.

"I have a list of places I want to go," says Eliza. "Easier if it's just the two of us."

She still seems uncharacteristically happy. Then I look at the others. My eyes meet Kendall's. She's studying my face.

The waiter comes to collect the check.

"You guys head outside," I suggest. "I'll wait for the change."

"Me, too," says Kendall.

After they leave, Kendall turns to me.

"If you don't want to spend the day with Eliza, don't spend the day with Eliza."

"I invited her."

"You regret it."

"Yes, I do. I was relieved when she showed up with other people."

"Then stay with us! Besides, we have three kindnesses left." Kendall smiles playfully. I wish so hard that we could be back where we were two days ago. With nothing but a city and a dare. Hours of pavement and conversation. Kendall's face framed by her blue stocking cap and auburn hair.

The restaurant door opens. Eliza peeks her head in. "Come on, Maxie!" she barks. Saying only my name, to make it obvious she's not saying Kendall's. She pauses for a moment, then closes the door again.

"I should go," I say.

Kendall shakes her head. "You're sad."

I slip on my coat. "I know."

She turns and leaves the restaurant. I hang back. Through the window, I see her step into the middle of Jamie, Camden, and Ari. Watch them move off together, leaving Eliza standing alone.

Then I go out to fulfill my duty.

"So," I say when I get out onto the sidewalk. "Where to?"

"Can we go to Times Square? So I can say I was there on New Year's Eve. Nobody has to know it was at two in the afternoon."

I can't help but laugh. "It'll be our secret shame." We start walking, and as we maneuver around a snowbank I ask, "So, tell me more about your Christmas."

"Max, you don't have to ask me these questions. Like you

have a list of what's safe territory for your ex-girlfriend."

"What if I actually, truly want to know the truth. How was it, *really?*"

Eliza sighs. "Of course, it was shitty."

"Your mom?"

"My mom, my dad, the whole stupid holiday. If it weren't for all the money I get, I would skip the whole thing."

"I thought your mom had been going to meetings."

"She has been. But she hasn't been completely sober, either."

I stop so suddenly that Eliza bumps into me. "Has she been, you know?"

"She slapped me once," says Eliza. "I slapped her back."

"You did not."

"I did."

Eliza's mother is an alcoholic. When Eliza's mother drinks, she hits Eliza. Her father knows about the drunk part, but not about the hitting. Eliza's never told him, because she knows he would leave her mom. Which would pretty much kill her. Despite the hitting, Eliza doesn't want a dead mom. She's always said she can handle it. I'm not so sure.

The light changes and we continue on.

Eliza takes my hand and asks lightly, "Are you seeing anyone?"

"When would I have an opportunity to date? I'm living at home and working as many hours as I can to earn money for school." I don't mention that this is a situation indirectly caused by her.

"Maybe you should stay at your grandfather's," she says. "Get a job in the city until the fall."

"I think that would hurt my dad's feelings. He likes having me around to help out with stuff."

She's silent for a moment, then says, "Is that really true? Or is that just an excuse?"

"What do you mean?"

"You're eighteen and you seem scared to death about starting your life."

"I'm not scared. My life starts in September. At Brown."

"How about sooner than that?"

"I didn't think you wanted to get rid of me so quickly."

Eliza freezes and pushes me, with both hands, sideways. "Enough of that! Max, I never asked you to defer college!"

"I know."

"Then stop blaming it on me!"

In a tumble of clarity, I see I've been completely wrong. Wrong to invite Eliza here, wrong to think she needed to see me, wrong to think I had anything to offer her. Maybe this is why she seems so different. She's grown up a bit. Evolved, while I've stayed the same.

"Okay," I say. Like a moron. Like a child.

We're here now. Times Square. It's already packed. The barricades are up. The cops are plentiful. Eliza raises her face to the nearest video billboard and squints at it like it's a new version of the sun.

"Ah!" she says. "The beating heart!" She loops her arm in

mine. We wander around a bit, letting the river of people push us one way, then another.

Someone's built a family of snowmen in the street. These are high-end snowmen. Expertly carved figures that almost look fake. I wonder how early someone had to get out here after the blizzard, to build these before the snow turned black and useless. It was a strange act of grace to create the snow sculpture and then leave it for people to discover.

Eliza goes over and gives one a hug.

Something is up, for sure.

Kendall

CAMDEN LEADS US TO A BUS SHELTER, CONFIDENT
that if we hop on the next one it'll take us where we want to
go, but I hang back.

"Do they know about what happened?" I ask Jamie.

"I told them, yeah."

"Would I seem like a total freak if I refused to get on a bus?"

Jamie looks squarely at me. "No, of course not. But I think
you should tackle this particular issue right now. If I can get
on, so can you."

He's right and I know it. I look to Ari and she just nods, and
then here comes a bus, so there's that added pressure.

"Okay," I say, and take a deep breath.

The bus squeals to a stop and I focus on keeping my eyes straight ahead of me, because if I do that I can't see the street and picture Luna there. Still, I hesitate before taking that first step on. Then another, and another, and suddenly I'm on the bus and it's moving.

It's crowded, so we stand. Jamie gets stuck a few people away from me, but Camden and Ari hang on to the same pole. They lean into each other, he circles her waist with his arm, and they both shoot me an identical concerned look. Ari offers a questioning thumbs-up.

I answer with my own thumbs-up, which will stay up as long as I don't imagine all the things in front of the bus that can be hit by the bus.

An older woman gets on, laden down with shopping bags. A guy wearing headphones gets up for her, offers her his seat. She nods once in a really businesslike manner, then sits. I know this gesture is part of an unwritten code of easy-peasy kindness, but still. There's something simple and beautiful about it, like a reliable miracle.

At the next stop, a seat opens up and Jamie motions for me to take it. I do, then he drops his messenger bag onto my lap.

"Just for a second," he says, smiling mischievously. He reaches into the bag and this feels intimate, awkward, until he pulls out a camera. It's not his big one with the expensive lens. This one is small and funky looking and could totally be a toy.

"My Holga." Jamie adds, "Lightweight and perfect for the city, in more ways than one."

He starts taking pictures through the bus window and I can't tell what's catching his eye. Maybe nothing, maybe just the city itself. I think back to all the photos we exchanged over the last few months, and it suddenly occurs to me: almost all of my photos were of people, while almost all of his were of buildings, signs, or landscapes. At the time, it felt like a conversation . . . but what if we were simply talking at each other without listening?

To pass the ride, I look around the bus at the faces of the passengers and begin assigning names in my head, starting with the guy across from me, who is positively, definitely Norman.

Eventually, Camden shouts, "We should get off at the next stop!"

We do, and when the bus pulls away, there's the arch of Washington Square Park. Jamie aims the Holga at the arch and starts snapping. Camden waits for him, but Ari tucks her arm into mine and we start crossing the street.

"Between his photos and your characters, you guys make quite the team," says Ari.

"At least we don't run around the county fair wearing costumes," I reply, and Ari smiles knowingly. She and Camden were into cosplaying an old sci-fi series last summer, and I wonder if that's still a thing for them. I've been so out of the loop, I don't know anything about their relationship now. How often do they see each other? Where do they spend time? Have they had sex?

"Have you and Camden had sex?" I blurt out.

Ari laughs, nervous. "Uh, sort of."

"What does that mean?"

"Not really."

"Okay. Well, I did."

"Did what?"

"Had sex."

Ari grabs my elbow and we freeze. "First of all, why are you bringing this up right now? And second of all, WHAT?"

"I guess I was eager to tell you," I say.

"Where did this happen? With who?"

"Ireland. His name was Declan."

"Okay." She pauses. "Go, Ireland."

"I wasn't ready to tell anyone. It seemed weird to email you to announce the evaporation of my virginity."

"*Evaporation of my virginity.* Nice. That would make a good album title," says Ari.

"Or a book," I add. "God, I missed you."

I pull her aside and we sit on a park bench. Jamie and Camden have walked through the arch now and we watch them. Jamie stops, positions his camera to get a shot of a tree. I tilt my head sideways to figure out what might be special about it but it's just a tree, spindly and naked and bored.

Ari's staring at me, studying my face, and I wonder what she sees. I wonder what looks different (hopefully something looks different).

"It was great, right?" she asks. "Your trip?"

"I can't really use single adjectives to describe it." I also feel like the more I talk about it, the more sparkle it loses. "But basically, being able to learn stuff without being stressed out about papers and tests, well, that was everything."

"I got that from your blog."

"You read the blog?"

"Duh. Why wouldn't I?" Ari smiles. "Although I was worried when you stopped posting. I had to check with your mom to make sure you were still alive."

"I got busy," I say. But Ari knows me, which means she knows I stopped posting because I simply stopped. Because I stop everything, after a while. If my best friend, who gets mostly As and works in her family's art supply store and babysits her little half sister, judges me for this, she never lets on. I have always fit in with her, even though on paper we shouldn't click together so easily. God, I'm so happy to see her right now, today, tonight, and at the beginning of next year.

Camden and Jamie crack up about something, and Ari and I watch them some more, because we can't not watch two boys laughing, especially if they're two boys we've kissed.

Then I ask Ari, "What happens to you guys after graduation?"

She winces and takes a deep breath. "Don't know. Camden's not interested in any of the colleges I am, except for one. Some are near each other, some aren't. We've decided to apply to whatever we're going to apply to and see how it shakes out."

They're on the edge of everything changing, and this may be a selfish thought but I don't care—I'm relieved that I'm not the only one who doesn't know what happens next.

Here comes Jamie.

"Wanna walk with me?" he asks.

I nod and stand up, and he flashes me this delicious grin before I follow him deeper into the park.

He's one thing that will happen next. That's way more than enough.

Max

I SPOT THE COUPLE WHILE ELIZA AND I ARE WAITING
for a light to change. They're youngish, in their twenties maybe.
Wearing similar parkas and gigantic backpacks. He's got a
guidebook, she's got a phone. Arguing at an empanada truck
in a language that sounds like it hurts your throat.

Arguing, like Luna and the guy. The kind of arguing that
makes you smile at first, because let's face it, it's funny. Funny
to get a peek at how couples talk to each other when they're
mad. Funny because, oh phew, you're not alone. It's a universal
truth: sometimes people in a relationship act shitty to each
other.

In this case, though, it's not serious. Not scary. I can see it in the way she rolls her eyes at him. The way he lets out a long, frustrated sigh. I step closer to them and hold my hand up in a half wave.

"Excuse me," I say. "Are you two okay? Do you need help?"

Eliza's confused. I feel her tug questioningly at my coat sleeve, then let go. I know this isn't fair. She doesn't have any context about the dare with Kendall. But I make a split-second decision not to tell her.

The guy frowns, shakes his head. Motions with his hand. A *be gone* type of gesture that should be enough to make me exit the scene, swearing at them under my breath. But the woman nods eagerly.

"I speak English," she says. "He doesn't. We need help, yes."

"What's the problem?" I ask.

"We are trying to go to the High Line. My husband says, we must go all the way down here." She shows me a map on her phone. Points to a dot labeled *Whitney Museum*. "But I say no, we can walk across and find it here, yes?" Her finger travels up to Thirty-Fourth Street.

"Well," I say. "You can start from either end. But personally, I like the north end. You can't see it on the map but it goes out onto an old pier. Nice view of the river."

I only know this because three months before my grandmother died, when she'd started a new drug that made her feel great for about a day, she took me to that pier. We leaned against the railing and watched a cruise ship head out to the ocean. We didn't talk. She just rested her hand over mine on the railing. It's one of my favorite memories of anyone ever.

"Ah, so I am right!" the woman says. "Then we walk, yes? That way for a few streets, then down?"

"Yes. Or you could take the subway."

The woman shakes her head. "No subway. Too confusing."

Her husband says something to her, his voice filled with disgust.

"You've never been on the New York subway?" asks Eliza.

The woman shrugs. Now I see she's embarrassed.

"Why don't we take you?" I hear myself saying. "The station's right there and it's a quick ride."

The woman looks me up and down, then Eliza. Checking for some ulterior motive, I'm sure.

"It's okay?" she asks. I'm not sure what "it" truly is, but I nod.

The woman speaks to her husband, and he really gives us the once-over. I've been scanned less thoroughly at airports. He asks her a question.

"Do we have to pay you?" she translates.

"No, not at all. This is just something nice."

"Something nice," she says, trying out the words. She repeats them (I think) in her language. Her husband scowls.

I can't explain it, but it feels extra important to finish the dare now. Without Kendall. On my own.

I point to the subway entrance across the street. When I start walking, the others follow.

* * *

Now we all get to wait awkwardly on a subway platform. The woman looks nervous. She keeps shuffling her feet and can't seem to stand still. Gosh, it's only a train traveling in tunnels under the ground. Get a grip.

"I'm Max, by the way," I offer. "And this is Eliza."

"I'm Kerstin," the woman says.

"Aksel," says her husband. No eye contact. He pretends to be fascinated by a Food Network poster.

"Where are you from?" I ask.

"Munich," Kerstin replies. German. *Duh!*

"First time in New York?" asks Eliza.

"For him, yes," says Kerstin. "I came here as a teenager. I lived with a family in Connecticut for one year."

"An exchange student?" I ask.

"Yes," she says, smiling. "It was a great time."

I almost say, *A friend of mine just spent a semester in Europe,* but catch myself. As another painful silence settles over us, I furtively send a text message to Kendall. I tell her I have Kindness Number Five covered, details to come.

A train comes and we step on. I spot two seats and motion for Eliza and Kerstin to take them. Aksel stands facing away from me, his backpack in my face. Charming. We ride in silence toward the Hudson Yards station.

Kerstin shoots her husband dirty looks the whole time. She doesn't appear at all nervous anymore.

Once we're back on the street, there are signs directing people to the High Line. We could leave Kerstin and Aksel here and I'd feel like I could check this one off. But we keep walking. Nobody talks.

Finally, we're climbing the steps to the raised walkway of the High Line. The pier stretches off in one direction toward the Hudson, the walking path lined with piles of snow.

"Well," says Kerstin, turning to me. "We are here, and I rode the subway. Are you always such a nice boy?"

I'm sure she doesn't mean to sound like she's talking to a puppy, but the words *nice boy* make me cringe.

"Max is the nicest person I know," says Eliza.

Kerstin takes off her gloves, reaches one hand into the other arm's coat sleeve. She struggles with something. When she pulls her hand away, it's holding a woven bracelet with a single onyx bead.

"I make these," says Kerstin. "I'd like you to have one."

I hold out my hand and let her drop the bracelet into my palm. Open my mouth to say *thank you*.

Before I can do that, someone hits my hand, knocking the bracelet into the snow.

"Stop it!" shouts Aksel, the words thick as smoke. Followed by a whole lot of extra-angry-sounding German.

Kerstin steps forward and slaps his hand the way he slapped mine. She shouts at him. It's unnerving, not knowing exactly what she's saying. She pauses, then speaks again, more slowly.

Aksel's face freezes when she says this last thing. There's a long pause where I wish Eliza and I could teleport out of the situation to anywhere else. A tropical beach, or even the dentist's office. Now Aksel simply turns and stomps away. Back to the staircase, back down toward the street.

Kerstin watches him, her eyes filled with tears.

"Are . . . are you okay?" I ask.

She looks at me. "Thank you again," she says, then heads toward the river.

Eliza and I watch her go.

"What the fuck was that?" asks Eliza.

"I have no idea," I say.

There's a terrible heaviness in the pit of my stomach. Eliza doesn't believe in regret, so she won't understand. Somehow all that was a mistake.

I don't know how or why, but in my efforts to be a *nice boy*, I made a bad situation worse.

Kerstin

I'M VERY SURE AKSEL'S ON THE PHONE AT THIS moment.

Talking to his girlfriend.

Yes, my husband has a girlfriend. And I just told him that I know.

What he did to that American boy was not from jealousy. It was from guilt. They are both the same to me, if it makes him look like a fool.

The thing Aksel still doesn't know is that I lied.

I don't refuse to use the subway because I'm afraid of getting lost. Why would I get lost? I've traveled to fourteen countries in ten years. Sometimes, when I'm out doing errands, I get lost on purpose for the fun of it. Also, I know how to use a map.

Aksel never questioned it when I told him I thought the New York subway was too confusing. I could tell he was pleased to find a weakness in me.

The real reason I don't take the subway in New York is because of what happened when I was seventeen.

I was visiting the city for the day, by myself, to go to a museum. Two men followed me up the steps in a subway station. One put his arm around my waist, while the other went for my bag.

I fought back.

One of my kicks was a good kick, and the man coming toward me lost his balance and fell on the stairs. Then they both ran.

I had bruises. But after that, I felt like I had escaped the one bad thing that was meant to happen to me, and from now on, nobody could hurt me. It changed me, that day. Sometimes, I am almost glad it happened.

So I didn't expect to feel so nervous on my first morning here with Aksel, when we started down the steps to a subway stop. It was the way the sound echoed. The U-Bahn in Munich doesn't echo that way. Only underground in New York do sounds echo that way.

When this boy offered to take us to the High Line, I was so surprised by the gesture, I said yes without thinking. Now I see it must be a sign, that I was ready to put that day behind me for good.

Maybe I am ready to put some other things behind me for good.

Aksel will call me in five minutes. I may as well set my watch now. He will say he's sorry, he will bring me a coffee. This is our pattern, this is our dance.

But I rode the New York subway again.

What if I didn't answer when he called? What if I sent Aksel home by himself?

I could get a job as a nanny for a family who wants their kids to learn German, or as a salesperson in a store that thinks my accent sounds sophisticated. I could stay at the hotel until I find a roommate. I could tell everyone I was staying in New York for a little while, and then never leave.

I have five minutes to decide.

Right now I'm just walking. Alone. And it feels, yes, very much all right.

Kendall

THERE'S A JAZZ TRIO PLAYING IN THE PARK, AND A small crowd's gathered around them. It's not frigid but it's not warm, so I'm surprised anyone's brave enough for busking today. But the city is packed and they'll probably make a fortune. Jamie stops to listen so I stop with him.

Even with the music it's my first quiet moment in a while, quiet enough for a Thought Worm to snatch the opportunity. What's Max up to right now? Did he tell Eliza about Luna and the dare and everything? What was the fifth kindness, and is it wrong for me to wish he hadn't done it without me?

"Hey," I say, crushing that Thought Worm and grabbing

Jamie's forearm. I don't feel like I can grab his hand again (yet). "Can we keep walking?"

He nods, then tosses a dollar bill in the empty guitar case in front of the jazz trio before we move on.

"So, what have you been up to these past few days?" he asks.

"Helping my brother move out of his apartment. Seeing *Wicked* with my mom. Walking around a lot." I pause. "I hung out with Max."

Jamie breaks his stride for a second, then regains it and asks softly, "What did you guys do?"

"We went to Central Park," I say, which is a truth. It sounds so simple when I frame it this plainly. "Mostly we talked about Luna."

This doesn't feel like a lie or even an exaggeration.

"Are you guys as freaked out about it as I am?" asks Jamie, his voice more relaxed now.

I pause. Why haven't we talked about this yet? "Yes," I finally say.

"Thanks for getting that info from the hospital," he says. "I wish I knew how she's doing today." His voice breaks down and I realize he's been struggling with this, too, but on his own. And he was the one who ran into the street, who knelt on the cold pavement next to her.

"We all wish that," I say, wondering exactly how many people I'm speaking for.

"I wish I could have done more."

"You did what you could. You were pretty awesome,

actually." Then, because I can't help myself, I add, "You did more than those of us who were standing right there."

Jamie frowns, shakes his head. "Don't beat yourself up about that. How were you supposed to know what was going to happen?"

I shrug. "We weren't. But maybe doing the right thing would have been a start."

That lands hard between us, and neither Jamie nor I have any idea what to do with it. Finally, Jamie holds up his camera and trains it at the dog park a few yards away. I am very familiar with this tactic. *When in doubt, take pictures.*

As I watch him, I think about what's going to happen later. Or rather, what I *want* to happen later. It's so obvious, it's almost painful. We'll kiss at midnight and then we'll continue. I won't stay in the city, I'll go home and back to Fitzpatrick, with a boyfriend. I'm already liking this plan.

We eventually circle back to the bench where Ari and Camden are waiting for us.

"Can we move on?" asks Camden.

"What did you have in mind?" I ask.

"There's a bakery in Little Italy I'd like to show you."

Jamie makes a *lead the way* gesture with his arm. Camden gets up and starts walking ahead of us. We follow.

I walk next to Jamie and after a block, he takes my hand.

Max

"SHOULD WE GO ALL THE WAY?" ASKS ELIZA.

"Beg your pardon?"

"All the way to the end of this thing," she adds with a teasing smile, pointing south. Toward the terminus of the High Line, blocks and blocks away.

"You tell me," I say, out of habit.

"No, you tell *me*."

This isn't like her. Eliza's someone who needs to be in control. She does this because the second she walks into her house, she's not in control anymore. But maybe the city is more my turf.

"The whole path is pretty cool," I say. "It takes a while but I think we should do it. You trust me?"

"Max, I'd follow you anywhere. You know that."

"Actually, I don't."

She grabs my arm, then stands on her tiptoes to kiss me lightly. (On the lips.)

"Silly Maxie," she says. "You always seem to know where you're going."

If this is true, I'm doing a great job of fooling the world.

"There's something different about you," I say.

Eliza stares at me. Swallows hard and almost nervously. Another un-Eliza-like move. "Is there?"

"Yes."

She shrugs and spins away from me. Starts walking. As always, I follow.

I first met Eliza when I was thirteen and she was twelve. She started at our tiny alternative school in the middle of the year and everyone was excited for a new student. Rumor was, she'd been pulled out of public school because she was being bullied. She had a total shell-shocked air about her, at first. And she was little. Like, short. The older girls took her under their wings, engulfing her so completely that I'm not sure I saw her at all that year.

The first time I really noticed her and how special she was, was in the school play the following spring. They were performing *Twelfth Night*. She was Viola and she was perfect.

But I was shy and not sure how to handle these growing limbs of mine. How would I ever be able to control two weird, long arms? Also, my feet knew I was clueless. They rebelled against me whenever they could, making me trip or lose my balance. I tried to keep my distance from the girls, but in a small school like ours, there's no room for that.

I watched Eliza date one boy, then another. Rumor had it, she also had a summer boyfriend. I dated, too, but at some point I was fully in love with her. Eventually, she was in love with me, too. At least, that's how she tells the story. Her story also says that we were always meant to be in each other's lives. When someone tells you a story enough times, it's hard to separate fact from fiction. Sometimes the fiction is all you need, when facts are confusing as hell.

Fact: It would be great if she met someone else, because maybe I could stop feeling guilty.

Also fact: I'll be devastated when she meets someone else, because she'll no longer need me.

I'm suddenly overcome with a strange sensation that I know how to destroy Eliza, if I wanted to: I could tell her about the past few days. Detail every hour Kendall and I spent together. Explain our dare and how it's already changed me. Eliza wouldn't know how to process all that. She'd see it as a betrayal, even though we are done and over.

It feels reassuring to have this in my back pocket.

We continue to walk south on the High Line. Eliza seems preoccupied with the buildings on either side of the walkway. Most of them are apartments. I can tell she's trying her damnedest to peek into them.

"This is the perfect place for an exhibitionist to live," she says, pointing to some windows across from us. "You could pull up all the blinds, dance around naked, and nobody could tell you not to because you're in your own house."

Eliza just laughs and starts walking again. Yeah, she is way too content. I catch up to her and put my hand on her shoulder. When she spins around, all I say is:

"Tell me."

Our eyes lock. I'm pretty sure I've got a real Stern Father thing going on my face. Her smile fades, but not completely. She bites her lip and makes a decision.

"I'm dating someone."

"Okay," I say. "Thought so."

Eliza scans my expression and I do my best to give her exactly the reaction she's looking for.

"You're happy for me, right?" she asks.

"Yes, of course." I pause, knowing what I have to do now. If I can make my mouth form the words, that would help. "Who is he? Someone from Dashwood?"

"No," she says as she shakes her head. Well, that's good. All the dating among our school population has a creepy inbreeding vibe sometimes.

"I'm not going to grill you. Whatever you want to tell me, I'll be glad to hear."

"Actually, I could use your advice," she says. Uh, yeah, that might have been the one thing I wasn't glad to hear.

"Sure," I say.

"Silas is great and you'd really like him. The thing is, he's older and he's offered to get me a fake ID so we can go out to bars together. Do you think I should let him cover it or should I insist on paying for it myself?"

"Older. How much older?"

"Thirty."

I stop walking and turn to her. "As in, thirteen years older than you?"

"Those are just numbers, Max. Jesus."

Eliza stands with her hands on her hips, daring me to stay upset about this. Am I overreacting? Is this no big deal if it's no big deal to her?

I think about her parents' strange relationship and I think about our strange relationship. I think about Luna and that guy. The way he was clearly used to having some kind of power over her. How she was trying to resist it. How much Luna reminded me of Eliza in so many ways. Not to mention the fact Eliza's still seventeen. A minor.

Yes. This is definitely a big deal. But I can't fight this battle with her right now.

"Insist that you pay him," I say, trying to keep my voice casual. "It sets up a good boundary."

Eliza nods, and we walk in silence for a little while.

"Why aren't you with him tonight?" I finally ask.

"He has to work. It's fine, waiters get great tips on New Year's Eve."

When she stops to visit a restroom, I type a text to Jamie.

Do you know Eliza's dating a guy who's 30?

My thumb hovers over the Send button. What's Jamie doing right now? I can't picture Jamie without picturing Kendall. Maybe they're wandering around some pocket of the city, taking photos and sharing moments. Hopefully, Kendall's happy. Getting what she's clearly wanted for so long. The image of a happy Kendall is a good one. She's smiling. The light in her eyes is on the highest possible setting.

Still, the thought of interrupting their good time is not an unpleasant one. Maybe I'm not the *nicest person* they know.

Which would be a huge fucking relief.

Kendall

THIS BAKERY ISN'T MUCH BIGGER THAN MY GROSET,
but smells a zillion times better. I huddle with Ari and Jamie at
a wobbly table in the corner as Camden brings us espresso and
a plate of powdered, sugary-looking lump-things.

"To this year and next year," he says once he sits, raising one
of the tiny white espresso cups.

We toast and I drink. Holy crap. I didn't know a year could
taste so bitter. But it's cool, our being here. I take a little photo
of it in my head and post it on an imaginary social media page
only I can see. *Look! You're doing something interesting with
people you like a lot!*

Jamie's phone buzzes and he digs it out of his pocket. When

he looks at the screen, he frowns a little, then puts it back in his pocket. Takes a sip of espresso. Then he takes the phone out of his pocket and stares at the screen again.

"Everything okay?" I ask.

"Yeah," he says. "Uh . . . my mom, asking annoying questions I don't know how to answer."

Jamie swivels in his seat so his back is to us and starts to type. Eventually he turns around, lets out a deep breath.

"Sorry about that," he says, flashing me The Grin. It's because of this grin that I'm in this micro-bakery right now. It's the grin I want escorting me into tomorrow and next year.

Something on the floor catches Ari's eye. She bends down and comes back up with a small flowered tote bag in her hand.

"Uh-oh," she says.

"I'm guessing that doesn't belong to those guys," says Camden, indicating the two super-old men at the only other table in the bakery.

I take the bag from Ari and peek inside. There's a wallet, makeup bag, and fat manila envelope. I pull out the wallet, holding it as gently as I can, as if showing someone, or maybe the wallet itself, that I mean no harm.

"We should give it to the guy at the counter," says Jamie. "I'm sure someone will come looking for it."

The guy at the counter looks like he wants to curl up somewhere and sleep for a week. I picture him emptying the wallet and tossing it in the trash. If he were a character, I'd name him Monty.

"Let's see if there's a name here," I suggest, opening the wallet. There's a little bit of cash, mostly dollar bills. I go for the cards and find a driver's license.

Shelby Dearden, it says. The address is in Brooklyn.

I dig some more. Shelby Dearden has loyalty cards for three different drugstores and two fro-yo places. This girl gets around. I dig deeper into the card compartment and underneath all of that, find a couple of business cards. *Shelby Dearden*, they say. *Member, Actors' Equity*. And there's a phone number.

"Aha!" I say, holding up the card.

Outside the bakery, where it's quieter, I dial the number on my phone.

"Hello?" a woman answers.

"Hi. My name is Kendall and if you're missing a bag, I have it."

There's a pause. "What kind of bag?" She sounds wary.

"A tote bag with flowers on it. It has your wallet and an envelope—"

"Oh my God!" she says. I hear rustling on the other end of the line. "I *am* missing a bag! I thought I'd slipped it inside a big shopping bag but it's not here. And you found it? Where did you find it?"

"At the Ambrosio Bakery," I say.

"I was there earlier. My God, that bag has a friend's play manuscript in it, with all my notes. I just got home to Brooklyn . . ." She pauses, and after a few moments of silence I wonder if we got disconnected. Then she says, her voice strange and soft now, "But I can come back. It would take me maybe forty-five minutes. Can I meet you somewhere?"

I look in the window of the bakery, at Ari and Camden and Jamie idly sipping their espressos. We are young and sort of stupid and planless and it's New Year's Eve. We have three hours to kill before we can go to Emerson's party. Finding a bag and not stealing its contents and calling the owner, that doesn't feel like a big enough kindness to count in the dare. That's just me, being raised well and acting on instinct. If I'm going to finish this, I want it to be with an action that feels deliberate.

"We're going to what?" asks Camden after I go back inside and tell them my idea.

"Go to Brooklyn. Bring this bag to its owner. Her name is Shelby."

"That's a long way for a good deed," says Ari. "Can't we just leave it here for her to pick up?"

I don't know how to explain to them that I need to do this. I believe in the universe poking us in the ribs, and I believe in the way Shelby Dearden's voice cracked out *Thank you* when I told her I'd bring the bag to her apartment. If he were here, Max would be totally on board and in fact, he might have suggested it, if I hadn't thought of it myself. I can see him, already on his phone looking at a subway map, navigating our route.

I can see him, and totally wish he were here, and wish I didn't wish that.

"Is this important to you?" Jamie asks.

"Yes."

"Okay. Then I'll go with you." He turns to Camden. "We'll meet you guys at Kendall's brother's place."

"Sounds good," says Camden, and I give him the address.

I gather up Shelby's things and put them back in the bag, arranging them the way they were when we found it. When Jamie and I step out onto the sidewalk, it really does feel different, being on our own without Ari and Camden. I can't decide if it's a good different or an awkward different.

"Shelby gave me directions," I tell him. "We head that way to the F train."

He takes my hand. I let that slight tug pull me closer to him, and then I kiss him on the cheek. It's quick, on purpose, because I don't want it to last long enough to take on meaning.

"What was that for?" he asks.

"For getting it," I say, and he lights up with a smile.

We eventually find the F train station but a train has just left. I lean against a stanchion and Jamie's phone rings.

"Hey, Max," he says as he answers, his voice suddenly serious. Then he takes a few steps away. I can still hear him perfectly. "Can we talk another time? . . . Yeah, of course I'm concerned. What do you want me to do about it?"

There's a pause.

"Me? Why don't you do it?"

Another pause.

"Yeah, but we have, like, five months left of school together. I don't want that kind of drama."

Jamie listens, then holds the phone away from his ear. Then he touches the screen to hang up and puts it in his pocket, walks back to me.

"That was Max, but we got disconnected."

"Uh, yeah, I just saw you hang up on him."

Jamie smiles. Shrugs. "Exactly."

The train thunders in.

It takes a while. After we leave Manhattan, I don't recognize the stations' names anymore. I open my notebook and start writing down names for the people, as if they were cats. Precious. Tiger Fluff. Misty.

Finally, we're off the train and climbing stairs into sunlight again, then we walk to Shelby's block. She said she lived in a basement apartment, which means one of those doors tucked underneath a brownstone's steps. All the windows on street level are barred, and I wonder if there was ever a time when they didn't have to be.

"Must be the next one," I say, pointing to the numbers on the buildings.

I step up to the door and touch my finger to the brass lion's head knocker. Fancy.

The door opens before I can use it, and there's Shelby Dearden. She's tall and blond and thin and striking. The kind of person who turns heads on the street, even in New York City. She's wearing a black cocktail dress and knee-high boots, and looks so fabulous a part of me instantly hates her.

"My heroes!" she says, smiling wide. "You must be Kendall. Come on in."

"Thanks. This is Jamie."

"Nice to meet you. Happy New Year."

Jamie and I step inside. The apartment looks like something out of a home furnishings catalog. A nice couch, a beautiful rug, puffed-up throw pillows, plus neatly framed photographs and art prints on the wall. The most unnerving thing is that Shelby Dearden seems familiar. Like, really familiar.

"I can't thank you enough for doing this," she says.

"Have we met before?" I ask. "I have a bunch of older brothers and I feel like maybe you know one of them."

Shelby laughs. "I certainly might. But I get that a lot, because of the commercial."

"Oh," I say.

"Tangy Ranch Crispo-Chips," she says, like that's a normal thing to just state, unattached to other things.

"Yes!" exclaims Jamie. "That ad is hilarious!"

In an instant, I can picture Shelby Dearden on a bus stop bench, a bag of Tangy Ranch Crispo-Chips in her hand. She's scarfing them down, getting crumbs all over her chin and clothes, and she's not wearing a black cocktail dress but a dingy sweat suit. A series of young, good-looking guys take turns trying to hit on her, clearly turned on by her chip-scarfing. That ad's been running for years and some people even quote it. No wonder she can afford a nice apartment in Park Slope.

"So you're an actress?" I ask.

"Trying to be. My career's sort of on hold at the moment."

Shelby tucks her long, shiny hair behind one ear and eyes the tote bag in my hand.

This is the horrible thing: Suddenly, I don't want to give it to her. Suddenly, I wish someone else had found the bag and stolen the eleven dollars out of it, then thrown the rest in the trash. Because women like her are used to others doing things for them, scrambling for their approval. That's the power attractive people have in the world. I bet she's had guys fighting over her in real life.

But I hold out the bag and she takes it.

"Again, I'm so grateful," says Shelby. "You have no idea how much it means to me that you came all the way here."

"No problem," I say, keeping my voice flat. Letting her know her powers don't work on me. "We should probably be going now."

Shelby nods, but looks sad and her lower lip pouts. "You're welcome to stay for a bit. My upstairs neighbor's coming over for dinner. There's more than enough food for more guests."

Jamie's face lights up. "That would be . . ."

I grab his arm. ". . . Lovely, but we're supposed to meet up with some friends at a party."

Jamie shoots me a look. "We can go over whenever. There's plenty of time to hang here for a bit."

"I'd really like to thank you for what you did," says Shelby.

But I don't want to give up time on New Year's Eve so I can make Shelby Dearden feel better.

"I hope someday, someone does the same for me," I say, and rewrap my scarf around my neck. I'm hoping this is a polite, final no.

Jamie shoots me a look, then glances at Shelby, who does appear disappointed. Whatever.

"Can I take a selfie with you?" he asks her. "I'm a big fan of your commercial. And your chips."

Shelby laughs and nods. Jamie steps up to her and she puts her arm around him. They pose for a shot with Jamie's phone.

I'll ask Jamie to send the picture to me, so I have proof: one more kindness, right under the wire. He doesn't have to know I wish I hadn't done it.

He doesn't have to know it was a waste.

Shelby Dearden

TAKING THE TRAIN INTO DOWNTOWN MANHATTAN and back meant walking three blocks, standing on a train platform, sitting on a subway, walking a few more blocks, then repeating in the other direction.

That completely destroyed me.

When I got home, I actually had to get into bed and take a nap. I thought about staying there for the rest of the day, but then I thought about Alma. I invited Alma down for dinner specifically so I had a reason to be up, doing things. A reason to travel to Little Italy to get dessert from her favorite bakery.

I've just been so tired.

For months and months, I've been so tired. The kind of

tired where every part of your body is heavy, and slow, and requires effort.

I went on a raw foods diet to see if that helped. That was basically starvation. I lost weight. In the mirror, I saw someone wasting away, trapped by my own body in more ways than one. Everyone else raved about how great I looked.

The doctors are doing tests. Tests, tests, and more tests. In the meantime, I put on all my favorite clothes and a lot of makeup and good-smelling hair product.

My mother developed lupus when she was in her twenties and I'm pretty sure this is my inheritance.

I can't work until I'm better, but I can't feel better if I'm not working.

I'm ashamed to tell anyone what's going on, but then I get mad when they don't help. It's really messed up.

But those kids. They offered help and I took it and the world didn't end.

Maybe I can teach myself to ask for more.

Max

WHEN ELIZA SAID IT WAS A COSPLAY BAND, THAT
was no joke.

Her friend is the lead guitarist of an all-female band that dresses as male Marvel superheroes. She's tricked out her guitar so it has a Captain America shield on it. It's pretty impressive. Eliza watches the set from the front of the crowd, center stage. I stand in the corner and watch *her*, glad to be doing at least one really cool thing on New Year's Eve. That was part of what I loved about being with Eliza. She gave me experiences I never would have found on my own, because I'm me.

We've struck a deal: we'll stay for one set, then meet up with our friends at Emerson's party. That's another cool place I want to be, at the stroke of midnight. This feels important.

The other reason to join them, which I didn't share with Eliza: I have to talk to Camden and Jamie. In person. To figure out what to do about this thirty-year-old guy. Camden will know what to do. He volunteers at a teen crisis helpline, for fuck's sake.

Problem is, I already know what to do. I don't need someone with Camden's training. It's really very simple.

We tell her parents.

That's it.

Four words. It shouldn't be complicated. Except it totally is.

Making these four words happen means possibly saying good-bye to my relationship with Eliza.

When the first set ends, I find Eliza in the crowd and tap her on the shoulder. She turns, sees me, then vigorously shakes her head.

"No!" she says, like a little kid. She actually stamps her foot.

"We had a deal," I remind her.

"How about halfway through the second set?"

I give her a long look. She thinks I'm giving in. I can tell because she's smiling. Then I just say, "Bye and Happy New Year," and turn away. Walk toward the exit. She thinks I'm bluffing.

I'm not bluffing. I absolutely refuse to be bluffing.

Now I'm out on the street and the cold hits me like a wave of relief. I'm surprised by how glad I am to feel it. How pure and clean it is.

Thirty seconds pass. I'll give her thirty more.

I take a few deep breaths, watching the fog I make with them appear, then dissolve. When the door to the club opens and slams shut, I don't turn toward it.

"Fine," says Eliza as she steps up beside me.

No, nothing is fine. But I'm happy to let her believe otherwise for now.

As we walk toward Kendall's brother's new address, I play out a sequence of events in my head:

I call her parents. Eliza hates me. She never speaks to me again. I am free.

I'm okay with how that plays out. I'll call tomorrow.

But wait. What if I chicken out tomorrow? That sounds like something I would do.

So I'll call them tonight and ask them not to talk to her about it until tomorrow. After we've both come home. That buys me some time and doesn't ruin tonight.

I look at her now. She already seems over the fact that I made her leave the show. That's because I didn't.

Eliza is never anywhere she doesn't want to be.

At the warehouse-looking building that matches the address Kendall gave me, someone buzzes us up without even asking who we are.

"Let me guess," says the young guy who opens the apartment door. "Max and Eliza?"

"Let *me* guess," says Eliza. "Someone described us as a really tall guy and tiny girl."

The guy laughs. "Well, yeah. I'm Taj. Come on in."

He leads us into a space with brick walls and posts and beams. Huge windows line one side of the room. The wooden floors are dark and ruddy, like someone singed them with a flame. Aside from one huge sectional sofa, there's nothing else in the apartment.

"I just moved in," explains Taj. "Furniture delivery got held up by the blizzard. More room for partying, I guess."

A handful of people are gathered in the kitchen, eating food from takeout containers. There's Jamie, showing some guy his Holga.

And there's Kendall, leaning against the kitchen counter, writing in her notebook.

I'm trying to figure out what to say to her when she looks up at me. For a moment, I can't read her expression. I wonder if she's still disappointed and disgusted. Then she smiles wide and her eyes change shape and it's possible that her skin lights up, too. I feel like I've come home.

"Hey!" she says.

Before I can react, Jamie calls, "Max!" and comes over. "Sorry I couldn't talk earlier. Kendall and I were in the subway. We schlepped out to Brooklyn to return some woman's lost bag and you know who it turned out to be? The Tangy Ranch Crispo-Chips girl, from that commercial!"

I know exactly what commercial he's talking about. But I'm more interested in the rest of the story.

"You returned a lost bag?"

"Yeah, with a wallet. We found it in a bakery and Kendall insisted on bringing it to the owner in person."

I can't help but smile.

So, she scored one. I scored one. We have one final kindness left.

I look at Kendall again. She's writing furiously in her notebook. I think it's awesome that she can do this here. At an unfamiliar loft in New York City on New Year's Eve.

I really want to talk to Kendall about Brooklyn. And about Kerstin. And about Eliza. And everything, really, beginning with the dawn of creation and ending with the second that just passed.

But I have a bigger issue to deal with first. I pull Jamie into a corner.

"We didn't get to finish our conversation from earlier," I say.

Jamie glances at Eliza, who's already chatting up a bunch of strangers.

"Now?" asks Jamie. "Can't we figure it out tomorrow or any of the other days that aren't New Year's Eve?"

"Figure what out?" says Kendall, appearing out of nowhere.

"Nothing," says Jamie curtly. Dismissively. I find myself enraged by this.

Kendall looks hard at me with those eyes of hers that are always so, so clear. The rush of what we discovered together comes over me.

I take her hand and lead her away from the others. To where, I'm not sure. Are there any rooms in this loft?

I find a door, open it, pull her in. The only thing in here is a mattress on the floor, and a sleeping bag on the mattress. I close the door before Jamie or anyone else can follow.

"What the F is going on?" asks Kendall.

"It's Eliza."

She sighs. "Oh my God. It's *always* Eliza."

"She's dating a thirty-year-old guy."

Kendall raises her eyebrows, but then scrutinizes my face. "That sounds like you just being jealous."

"I'm not jealous. I'm concerned."

"Don't you think Eliza can take care of herself? I'll bet she's capable of bossing around a boyfriend twice her age."

"It's not okay, Kendall. She's not even eighteen. He wants to get her a fake ID and sounds like a total creep." Then I pause. "And it makes me think of Luna and that dude."

"That's not fair," says Kendall. "Playing the Luna card."

"Sorry," I say. "But I have a bad gut feeling about this. Right now I'm standing on that street corner and everyone else is afraid to do something."

I hope Kendall gets it. She must. She's the only one who can.

And she does. I watch her face change.

"Jamie doesn't want to deal with it right now," I continue. "Camden would, but I can't get ahold of him and I'm not sure when he's going to show up. I need to do this before midnight. I can't explain it, it's just important to me."

Kendall simply nods. "We do need one more, for the dare."

"Forget the dare! Besides, Eliza's not a stranger."

"Okay," she says. "So call her parents right now. I'll stay here and make sure you do it."

I didn't realize I wanted her to offer exactly that, until she did.

There's a knock on the door.

"Hello?" says Kendall.

"Oh, good." It's Jamie's voice. "I was wondering where you went. You okay?"

"Yes," she says. "Just have to make a call."

"Do you know where Max is?"

She pauses. "I think he went looking for the bathroom."

Footsteps move away.

"Take out your phone," Kendall says with a chin-nudge. "Call them."

I do as I'm told.

Dial Eliza's home number.

It rings once.

I hang up.

"What was that?" asks Kendall.

"I don't know. My fingers panicked."

"Your *fingers*."

"I need a moment."

"I'm not getting this. You desperately need to call, but you desperately need more time, too."

"That's exactly right."

"Explain."

How to do that?

"Making the call means letting her go," I say.

Kendall's quiet for a second, then simply nods. "It might not mean that."

"I like to be prepared for the worst-case scenario."

I hold out my phone again, hover over the words *Eliza Home* on the screen.

Then I put my phone down again.

"Oh, for Christ's sake," says Kendall. "If you don't, I will."

I don't know why I didn't think of this before.

Kendall can call. Kendall has nothing to lose. Kendall and Eliza already hate each other.

"Would you?" I ask.

And I hold the phone out to her.

Kendall

WHY SHOULD I DO THIS? FOR HIM? FOR *HER*?

If I do this, I'm really sticking it to Eliza, which has definite appeal.

But also, in my heart, despite how I feel about the person in question, I know it's the right thing to do. Plus, I'm going to go ahead and count this in the dare. Eliza and I are more than strangers, we're enemies. Shouldn't the last kindness be for someone like that anyway? Let's finish this thing with a bang.

I take out my phone.

Max fills me in on the details of what he knows, so I can share them with Eliza's parents.

"Make sure they're both on the line," says Max. "Or at least Eliza's dad. If it's just her mom, we'll try again later."

Max shows me the number, and I dial it and it's ringing now, and my heart's pounding.

"Hello?" answers a voice. Eliza's mom, I assume. She sounds bored. I picture an older version of Eliza, lounging on a fainting couch.

"Hi. Is this Eliza's mom?"

"Yes. Who is this?"

"My name's Kendall. I'm a friend of hers." Already with the lies.

"Well, hello, Kendall," she says. Overly friendly, because she thinks she's supposed to know me but she can't remember, so she's going to fake it.

"Is Eliza's dad home, too?" I ask.

There's a pause. "Why?"

"I have something to tell you, but I want to tell you both."

Another pause. "You can just tell me."

"Can he please come to the phone, too? If he's there?"

She exhales slowly, then I hear her call for her husband to pick up. That it's Eliza's friend and it's apparently important. *Apparently.*

A click, then a deep male voice. "Hello?"

I introduce myself. And then I do it. I tell them that Eliza has a new boyfriend and he's thirty and his name is . . .

"Silas," Max whispers.

And we, Eliza's friends, are concerned.

All this time, they're silent.

Then I hear a click. Silence again.

"Hello?" I ask into the void.

"I'm still here," says Eliza's dad. "My wife hung up. I believe she's upset."

"Oh. Sorry."

"Don't be sorry. You did something good, by calling us."

"I hope so," I say. He doesn't know the half of it.

"Eliza's lucky to have a friend like you," he adds.

Yeah, he knows less than half. More like an eighth . . . or maybe a twelfth.

But I simply say, "Thank you."

Then we're saying good-bye. When I hang up, I'm overcome with the sensation that I've performed a role in a short play that went off without a hitch.

Max is looking at me with a very strange expression.

"Oh my God," I say. "Are you going to cry?"

"No. I'm just . . . grateful. You didn't have to do that, but you did."

We're silent for a moment. The radiator in the corner clangs, and I find it strangely comforting that an apartment this trendy would still have a radiator that clangs. I take a deep breath, possibly the deepest one I've taken in days.

"I think maybe someday we'll be okay," I say. "About Luna."

Max closes his eyes and nods. Takes his own deep breath. "Yeah. Maybe we will."

Then he opens those eyes and sees right into me. I can feel

it. I want to wrap my arms around his neck and hug him for a long time, but on the other side of the door is the rest of the world and the rest of the world is waiting.

Instead, I open the door.

The rest of the world is not waiting, but Eliza and Jamie are.

Um, yeah, that's not good.

"You have got to be fucking kidding me," Eliza says, so slowly it's frightening.

I don't know what to do so I look at Max, but clearly, *he* doesn't know what to do, either. I think about closing the door, locking it, and barricading ourselves behind the mattress. Instead, I do nothing.

"You *called* my *parents* about Silas?" says Eliza, her voice suddenly raspy.

"It wasn't her," says Max.

"I just heard her talking to them!"

"I asked her to do it."

He steps in front of me.

"You?" asks Eliza.

"Yeah."

She spins and runs away, across the loft toward the front door.

Max starts to go after her, but there's Jamie, grabbing his arm. He shakes his head at us, his grip still firm on Max. "I'm totally confused. What's going on between you two?"

"Nothing!" I say, cringing at how defensive and weak it sounds.

"You wouldn't help me, so she did," says Max, not defensive and weak at all.

"It had to be tonight?" asks Jamie. His gaze settles on me, full of betrayal. "It had to be her?"

"Yes," says Max. It's the most badass, sure-of-itself, don't-fuck-with-me *yes* I've ever heard.

Jamie shakes his head. "Shit, Max. Haven't you messed up Eliza enough already?"

"What are you talking about? All I've ever done is *cleaned up* her messes."

"You're still around instead of at college. You invited her into the city to spend New Year's with you. Dude, don't you understand how confusing that is for her?"

Max opens his mouth to say something, but can't think of anything fast enough, I guess.

Jamie sighs, really pissed off now. "I'll go find her. Why don't you hurry up and get on with your life already?"

He stomps over to the front door, finds his coat and also Eliza's, then turns to me. Baffled and hurt.

"Are you coming back?" I ask him.

"I don't know," he says.

I nod.

Then he's gone.

Max

IF I GO NOW, I CAN FIX THIS.

I can catch up to them. Talk to Jamie and explain how much the thing with Luna jammed me up. How much Kendall helped me.

Once things are okay with Jamie, I can make things okay with Eliza. And even if I can't, at least I can make sure she's safe. Not wandering the city by herself at midnight. I can make sure she gets home tomorrow. I'll take her myself if I have to.

I start for the door.

Someone grabs my arm again. The same spot that Jamie grabbed, so it's still a little tender. This time, it's Kendall.

"What?" I snap at her.

"Don't go after them," she says.

"I have to."

"No, you don't."

"Kendall . . ."

"What you have to do, is you have to *stop*."

I shake her hand off my arm and step away. I'd like to sit, but there's nowhere to do that.

"Max," continues Kendall. "You said you were prepared to let her go. So do it!"

She's right, of course.

I look over at the door. I could still make this better. Before I can do or think anything else, Camden bursts through that door, holding a bottle of something high above his head.

Now here's Ari. "We made it!" she says. "Fifteen minutes to spare!"

I check my phone. Whoa. It really is 11:46.

Kendall grabs Ari and steers her into the kitchen. Pushes her toward Emerson, who swallows her in a hug.

"Don't worry," says Camden, waving the bottle at me. "This is sparkling cider."

Sparkling cider is the least of my problems. Camden sees this on my face.

"What? What is it?"

I pull him toward the wall and tell him what happened. All of it, unedited. When I finish, Camden looks at me for a long time with incredible sadness. For whom, I'm not sure.

Finally he says, "You did exactly what you were supposed to

do. Not asking Kendall to do it, I mean. But making the call. As soon as possible."

"Tonight?" I ask.

Camden nods without hesitation. "Tonight."

"Guys!" calls Ari as she and Kendall move toward us. "Emerson says we can go out on the roof!"

There's a minor stampede as the whole party pours out of the apartment. Into the hallway and up the stairs. Ari takes Camden's hand and starts to pull him into the rush. Kendall stands there looking at me. I stand there looking at her.

Then Ari and Camden circle back to us. Ari reaches out her other hand for Kendall's. Kendall takes it. Then the three of them are moving away from me. I wait for Kendall to glance back.

She doesn't.

I'm alone in the apartment now and there's nobody to stop me from leaving. I know exactly where Eliza's headed. Back to the club, back to her cosplay band friends. I could be there in ten minutes if I run.

Eliza

I KNOW MAX WILL COME AFTER ME, BECAUSE HE always does, does, does.

Let me whisper a secret in your ear: I don't want him to.

I'm pissed as all holy hell at the guy but also, thank goddess, he seems to have moved on.

We're in a Dunkin' Donuts because we couldn't get back into the club and Dunkin' Donuts is familiar and this one's open twenty-four hours. My buzz from the party has officially worn off. Coffee's the only thing for it now, along with a couple of chocolate Munchkins because, how else are you going to pretend you have giant alien eyeballs and try to make your companion crack up? But Jamie sits slumped with his head on his arms. He's mad at himself because in one moment he chose me, and our friendship, over a girl he's really into. It was a big moment, the kind you can't ever undo.

Oops for him.

Jamie's a good guy and a great friend, but he's indecisive and terrified of getting serious with someone. He liked her, then he didn't, then he didn't like how much he liked her. No wonder they clicked: she's indecisive, too. It's painfully obvious to everyone that she's in love with Max. Jamie will be okay, eventually. I'll help him find some other girl to scare the shit out of him.

Now here's another text from my dad. That makes four phone calls and seven texts, but who's counting? To hell with it. This one I'll answer.

Staying over with friends. Home tomorrow. I promise.

(Maybe.)

Part of me is glad they heard about Silas and freaked out. It's proof that they care.

Jamie raises his head, then plunks it back down facing the other way.

Yeah, he's terrible company but he's here with me.

Max, too, at least in spirit. I never *not* feel his support. And also, Camden's. People who loved me, people I let down, people I swirled up tempests for.

I hope I give them as much as I take. Because when I do reach whatever door comes next, I'll need them all to push me through it.

Kendall

HOLY CRAP, IT'S COLD UP HERE.

I watch Ari and Camden wrap their arms around each other.

If Jamie hadn't left, maybe he'd be doing the same thing and my teeth wouldn't be chattering.

I understand why he went after Eliza. Maybe he will actually come back and everything will be okay and perfect and at least a little warmer.

Someone puts their hand on the top of my head. I spin around.

But it's Emerson.

"You're shivering," he says.

I step toward him and he gives me a hug, and his breath

smells like cigarettes. I love my brother so much, even if he is a big idiot sometimes.

"I won't ask where your guy is," he says.

"Thanks. I won't ask where *your* guy is."

"It's going to be a great year, Kendall. You're going to rock your last months of high school."

With all the drama, I haven't had the chance to tell him about maybe not going back, but this isn't the time.

"Three minutes!" someone yells, and I hear a champagne cork being popped. Someone passes out plastic flutes.

I look up at the stars. Only the brightest, brashest ones are out.

Someone calls to Emerson to come get a glass and he moves away. I go to the railing of the rooftop deck, which faces west, toward the Hudson River. The lights of the city are scattered in patterns, random yet organized. From up here, they look like hope and magic and life itself. I think of Luna, and Erica the waitress, and the seven times we found a way to be truly kind to other people, and suddenly I don't feel like the spectator anymore. This isn't some giant photograph on a museum wall somewhere. I'm in this. I'm a part of it.

The Biggest Thought Worm Ever arrives:

Where I belong is here, because that's where we *all* are, fighting our hard battles for the same things.

The force of realizing this makes me tear up. Or maybe it's the wind.

Emerson hands me a champagne, then moves off. I silently toast anything (The new year? Erica's dare? Myself?) and take a small sip and the bubbles warm me up.

"Thirty seconds!" someone yells, maybe the same someone as before but maybe not.

Ari and Camden have found a spot against the railing. Their foreheads are touching and they're talking intensely about something good, I can tell. Maybe he's telling her he loves her or maybe she's telling him that whatever happens next, it'll all work out.

Suddenly, the crowd is counting down from ten.

Nine.

Emerson's nowhere to be found.

Eight.

Jamie definitely did not come back.

Seven.

I check my phone. He didn't text, either.

Six.

This is really not how I imagined tonight, at all.

Five.

How is Luna right now? What is she thinking? I picture a nice nurse holding her hand.

Four.

Maybe it's time for me to go. I walk toward the door.

Three.

I reach for the handle, throw it open.

Two.

Christ, what a relief to step back into the stairwell, out of the wind.

One.

"Kendall?" asks someone from behind me. I turn around.

Happy New Year!

"Max?"

He steps forward from a corner, right inside the door.

"Hey," he says, and in the mostly darkness I can see that he's smiling.

Before I know it, I'm throwing my arms around him. "I'm so happy you're here."

He laughs. "Me, too."

We look at each other and his face is draped in shadows, so I imagine that mine must be, too. Outside, I can hear people blowing horns.

Now it happens. My lips on his, and I'm surprised by how much I remember about them. There's a boom of fireworks from somewhere out there in the cold, non-Max-kissing world.

Max pushes me gently against the wall. It's good to have this foundation suddenly, something to keep me upright. I look up above the door and see the red glowing exit sign, and wonder what it must look like to someone scrambling down the stairs in a fire.

He pulls away. "Did you know we'd end up here?" he asks.

"No," I say truthfully. "But I think maybe I wished for it."

Max shakes his head. "Why is this always happening under

the most fucked-up circumstances?"

"I don't mind the fucked-up circumstances," I say, taking his hand. It's smooth, but cold, and the sheer size of it makes me like him even more. It's like grabbing a lion's paw.

"Where is Jamie?"

"Don't know. Will you come with me onto the roof? It's beautiful out there."

The fireworks have ended and now we just hear people singing, badly and drunkenly, from the other side of the door. It's really important to me, suddenly, that we get on the other side of the door. Like, that's where the new year and pretty much everything else starts.

Max nods and I still have his hand in mine, so I push on the bar and the cold air rushes in, and then so does reality. We step onto the roof and the first person I see is Ari, her gaze locked on our joined-hands situation. She smiles with one side of her mouth.

I lead Max to the other end of the deck, away from all the others.

We take in the night. The lights, the shapes of the buildings, the hum of the city churning forward. Max reaches for my cheek and turns my face to his, and we kiss again. Slowly, gently, like we're already old pros at it. Like we have all the time we could possibly want to do this.

"What now?" asks Max.

"You tell me," I reply, passing the buck.

"We'll go home. I'll start my job again. You'll go to school.

We'll have the rest of winter and spring and summer."

When he says *summer*, I picture our town's swimming lake, and the creek where I know Max and his friends like to hang out. I see the Ulster County Fair and mini-golf at the Scoop-N-Putt, where I always work from June to August. It unrolls like a tapestry in my head.

Maybe because I'm thinking about a much warmer situation, I shiver uncontrollably. Max opens his coat and he doesn't have to ask me twice, I step into him and he wraps his coat around me tight, tight, tight. I slide my arms around his waist and dig my hands into his back jeans pockets. This is really intimate and rather fresh, but I don't care. I feel like this is a small concession to wanting to put my hands everywhere on all six feet plus of him.

In one pocket, my hand hits something sharp with corners.

"Is that an envelope in your pocket, or are you just happy to see me?"

Max snorts and nuzzles my neck. Oh my God. *Do that again! Better yet, do it forever!*

"Ha-ha. Something Big E gave me earlier. I forgot I had it."

"Aren't you going to open it?"

"He likes to give me magazine articles. I'll open it later."

I grab the envelope and pull it out, then bring it around so it's between us.

"Open it now! Maybe it's something funny."

"I can pretty much guarantee it's not."

"Read the headline, at least. Then we can call this year the

'Year of' whatever the headline is."

Max smiles and shakes his head. "You're crazy, but you're cute."

"It works for me," I say with a smile, so glad we get to do this again. To play, to spar, to simply have fun (and kiss a lot more).

Max opens the envelope, then removes a folded piece of white paper with handwriting on it. There's something else in the envelope, but I can't tell what it is. I look up to examine Max's frown, because this is not what he expected to find. In fact, he actually turns away from me and hunches his back against the wind.

"What?" I ask, trying to see.

"I can't believe it," he whispers.

"What?"

Max turns back around, his fist clenched around the paper, which he's folded tightly.

"Big E gave me an airline gift card. With a note saying he wants me to go to Seattle."

"Okay. That's . . . random."

"Well, my uncle invited me to come there before I start college. I can stay with him and do an internship at his tech company, and travel. I didn't think anyone knew about it."

I have no idea what to say to this, and this new possibility of Max being gone and not with me.

"I'm a little blown away," continues Max. "Too bad I can't accept the gift."

Max stuffs the envelope safely back into his pocket and reaches for me. He kisses me deeply and it's almost enough to make all the Thought Worms stop their frenzy in my head.

There's one for the many months I just saw playing out, me and Max and school and home. Him giving me whatever I need to get through my final semester.

There's another Thought Worm for how much Max regrets putting off college for Eliza.

Max regrets! the Thought Worm squeals.

It's almost loud enough to make me open my mouth and say something similar to him.

Suddenly, I hear Ari's voice call, "Guys!"

We turn and there's Ari and Camden moving toward us, together.

"Happy New Year!" says Ari, and they're wrapping their arms around us until we're in a four-way hug.

I close my eyes and let the sound of the wind drown out all that noise inside me.

Max

ON THE SUBWAY, KENDALL AND I GRIP THE SAME
pole, our bodies pressed close. Foreheads touching.

The train will stop any second at Seventy-Seventh Street.
It's where I get off. Kendall, Ari, and Camden will continue on,
to crash at Emerson's now-ex-boyfriend's apartment. Beyond
that, I have no idea what comes next.

"This is me," I say as the train slows. What else should I
add? *I'll call you! We can go on an actual non-fucked-up date!*
I really want to kiss her good-bye, but feel suddenly shy about
that.

Kendall nods, her eyes wide. They dart around us, asking
questions. Searching for answers.

The subway doors hiss open and I let go of the pole. Step backward with my hands raised in the lamest farewell gesture ever. Then I blink hard and turn around. Leap from the train onto the platform.

The train pulls away and I'm bereft again. This is what it felt like in the lobby of Taj's apartment building. I couldn't leave. I couldn't leave *Kendall*. It's why I turned around and rode the elevator straight back upstairs.

Fortunately, by some miracle, Kendall's standing on the platform next to me. I almost jump when I see her.

"Not yet," she says. "Not like that."

Thank God.

I smile and hold out my hand. She takes it. We step forward.

When we get to Big E's building, we still haven't said anything to each other. I haven't really even looked at her face since the last block, because when I did, she looked confused and upset.

"Happy New Year," I say to Tony in the lobby. He echoes it back. It's cool to have this simple, one-size-fits-all thing everyone can communicate to everyone else.

In the elevator, Kendall stares at the security camera mounted in the top corner. She squints at it, as if trying to see something inside.

Big E's asleep when we enter the apartment, *New Year's Rockin' Eve* on the TV. I still can't believe his gift. I wonder when he got it. It must have been before Christmas, before our time together here. I wonder if it took him a while to decide to give it to me.

Kendall walks ahead, straight to my room. I follow her. Which should feel strange, since this is not her turf, but it doesn't feel strange at all. Once we're both inside the room, I close the door. Glance once at Freddie Mercury, who seems much less pissed off now. He seems psyched for us, actually. Kendall sheds her coat and moves toward me.

We kiss for a long time. Let me just say, when you've only kissed someone in weird settings, kissing in the normalcy of a bedroom feels like a whole extra level of amazing.

I step out of my coat. Off with our boots. Now we're on the bed. There's a red glowing question mark in the back of my head. What does she want? What does she expect? Those questions apply to me, too.

"Just so you know," says Kendall, drawing away from me, her breath jagged. "I'm not having sex with you. Not here, not tonight."

"Okay," I say. "Good." Now I know that's what I want, too. My brain does at least. My body will come around eventually.

"I wanted more of tonight, that's all. Even if it's time while we're asleep."

"Are you tired?"

"No way."

"Me neither."

Still, we lie down on the bed. She fits perfectly into the crook of my arm, her head on my chest.

I feel like this is where we're supposed to talk. To open up, share our secrets. Thing is, we already did all that. Maybe now, it's time to simply be together. Many minutes pass. I'm pretty sure she's asleep. I start to drift off myself.

"Max?" comes Kendall's voice, piercing the silence.

"Mmmm?"

She pauses. She really wants to say something, I can tell. It's a struggle to stay conscious enough to hear it.

"Never mind," she says.

My eyes fall closed again. All I feel is exhausted and the true existence of her next to me.

In the morning, I'll be ready to be whatever person she needs.

JANUARY 1

Max

WHEN I WAKE UP, IT'S LATE. I CAN TELL FROM THE
light leaking through the shades.

It takes a few seconds for it all to rush back in and I turn to Kendall, already smiling.

But she's not there.

I prop myself up and look around the room. Her coat and boots are gone, too.

The envelope from Big E sits on the night table. She's written on the back of it.

If you don't use this and stay here because of me, you'll always regret it. I don't want to be part of that.

We'll be doomed from the start. Go to Seattle. Have an amazing time. Please don't call or text or anything for a while, it'll make this so much harder than it already is.

I loved these last few days. Call me when you get back.

Happy New Year.

K.

I read the note three times, trying to make sure I understand what's happened. And why. And also trying to understand what I feel.

Which is, set free. This freedom is terrifying but now I know how much I wanted it.

I'm going to Seattle.

Everything between now and September looks completely different. It looks the way it should.

I close my eyes and imagine Kendall in my arms, her hair in my face, and know that will have to be enough for now, and for a while, and maybe for good. That hurts, but it's not a bad hurt.

When I can finally venture out into the living room, Big E is awake, watching the news. I sink down into the chair next to him. After a minute of us simply sitting there, he mutes the TV and turns toward me.

"Thank you," I say. "For the . . . envelope."

He stares at me for a moment. The slightest twitch of a smile on his lips. "Your father told me about the invitation to

Seattle. He also told me you were being an idiot and convinced yourself you had to stay here and earn money for tuition."

"That's all true."

"Whatever you and your dad can't cover, I will."

"Big E . . . you don't have to—"

"Of course I don't fucking have to. Are you going to use the card?"

"Yes."

"Great. When are you leaving?"

"I don't know. I have to figure some things out first."

"Like what?"

I open my mouth to answer, and realize I have no idea how.

"I guess I could call Uncle Jake today," I finally say. "And I could leave right away. Maybe even tomorrow."

My grandfather searches my face. For what, I don't know. But for the first time in a long time, maybe ever, I think maybe he'll find it.

"Good," he says. "Don't waste a single day if you don't have to."

Okay, then. Maybe I can actually do this. I get up and turn back to him one more time.

"I'll send you postcards, but you have to actually read your mail."

"I'm agreeable to that arrangement."

We're silent again. I know that any second, his attention is going to drift back to the TV. Or maybe it won't and he'll reach out to hug me. I'm not sure which would be worse.

"I have to go pack now," I say.

"Be gone, then." Big E waves his hand, as if I'm a pest and he wants me to scat. But he's full-on smiling now.

Be gone.

Yes. It's time for that. Funny thing is, I've never felt so present.

Kendall

ERICA'S WORKING THIS MORNING, LOOKING CRISP
and 500 percent more awake than anyone else in the coffee
shop. Honestly, it hadn't crossed my mind that she *wouldn't*
be working. I couldn't imagine her not being here, waiting for
Max and me to show up. Although as I slide onto a stool at
the counter, I realize it's very possible she's forgotten about us.
Maybe she throws out her dare to a dozen people a day.

I wait until she comes behind the counter to grab a pitcher
of coffee.

"Hi," I say, waving to catch her eye. "Erica, right?"

She smiles politely. Yeah, no way does she remember me.

"Good morning," she says.

"I was in here a few days ago with my friend. Super-tall guy?"

Erica squints as if trying to see into her own blurry past of customers.

"You gave us a challenge, to do seven acts of kindness to strangers before New Year's."

She puts down the coffee pitcher. "Yes. That's right."

"Well, we did them."

"You did them."

"All seven. We have proof."

Erica smiles for real. "Do you, now?" She looks off toward the tables. "Hold on. I'll be right with you."

She moves to one of the tables, refills several coffee cups, then returns, placing the pitcher gently back onto its warmer.

"Okay. I'm all yours." She leans her elbows on the counter, like she's waiting for me to tell her a story.

I pull out my notebook and I show and I tell. As I'm doing that, I realize that I've actually been able to finish something I started. It's not my novel about the end of the world but it's better, it's about the beginning of something, at least for me, filled with characters more interesting than anyone I could make up.

When I'm done, Erica just says, "Wow. I had no idea that you'd take me seriously."

"Well, we did."

"I promised you a fantastic breakfast, didn't I?"

I've thought about this.

"Yes, but my friend's not here and it wouldn't feel right to have it without him. Can you give it to someone today who seems like they need it?"

Erica laughs. "Sure, sweetie. That won't be hard, believe me. I promised you a photo on the wall, too."

"*That* I'll take you up on. Can I send you one to use?"

I show her the picture of Max and me at the penguin house. We look tense and awkward, like someone forced us to be there. We are not those people anymore. But I love that that version of us will live on the coffee shop wall: confused and lost, drifting our way through some kind of purpose while surrounded by the rest of the world. Not knowing, yet, what we were capable of. Not knowing that it would all come together at midnight.

Ari, Camden, and I grab the last forward-facing three-person seat on the Metro-North train, and this is important. I couldn't bear to ride backward, it would be too symbolic. But I am, after all that, going home and back to school. I am doing it because I know I can, or at the very least I know I can try and that's enough for now.

Ari and Camden let me have the window. Before the train's even left Grand Central, they're both asleep, Ari's head in Camden's lap, and I'll be honest, that stings. Because if I hadn't left Big E's the way I did, if I hadn't scribbled that note quickly before I changed my mind, Max and I might be doing something similar. Everything would be different.

But it would also be wrong.

Right should feel better than wrong but at this second, not so much. There are at least twenty different moments for me to replay in my head from last night with Max and let me tell you, every single one of them causes me physical pain.

Finally, we're on the move and as we travel out of the tunnel and north through Harlem, I'm determined to think about something else.

Jamie? asks a Thought Worm.

Okay. What about Jamie? I picture his face right before he ran after Eliza and expect to feel angry and guilty. But all I feel is relief. Every minute of being with Jamie took effort, and not that I have anything against effort, but when you experience a different way of being with a person, stuff begins to make sense. Jamie and I were never going to happen, at least not in any real or lasting way. It all went down the way it needed to, for him and for Eliza, too.

So I think about Luna. I open my notebook and sketch what I remember about her. I start with her eyes, and then her mouth. The rest is a little fuzzier in my memory, but I go on impulse.

Then it's time to start writing her up as a character. I scrawl her name, but when I try to write more, I find I can't do it. Instead, I add the word *Dear* in front of *Luna*, and now the words come.

I tell her about everything that happened in the days since she stepped off that curb. It takes me most of the train ride. My handwriting is shaky and it's a struggle to keep it legible. When I get home, I'll send this to the hospital and maybe she'll get it, maybe she won't. Maybe she'll be able to read it herself or maybe someone will have to read it to her. Maybe she can't even hear or understand it. These are things I have no control over.

I take a picture of the finished letter for extra proof that yes, I did this.

The Hudson River sparkles with midday light and when it does that, it's hard not to feel like maybe everything will be okay.

JANUARY 2

Max

A LAST-MINUTE TICKET MEANS GETTING STUCK IN
the middle seat. I'm not sure who seems more annoyed by my
presence: the woman in a tracksuit on my left by the aisle, or
Suede Vest Guy on my right by the window. I'm basically a
folded-up human accordion, my kneecaps pressing hard into
the seat in front of me. Every time the little kid in that seat
moves, it jiggles. Ow.

I check my phone again.

I don't know who I'm expecting to hear from. Everyone
went back to school today, including Kendall (I fucking hope
she went back to school today). It's ten thirty and I wish I knew
what class she has now. I wish I knew what she's thinking and

feeling and remembering. I start writing her a "good luck at school" text message . . . then stop myself.

Honor what she said about no contact, doofus. Be cool.

I lean forward to peek out the window. Outside on the tarmac, there's white snow and gray concrete. A pale silver sky beckons. No more of that palette for me, for a while. I'm going back to colors. Not the artificial holiday kind, but real colors. Ones that occur in nature. Especially green. Green goes a long way toward making you feel good about shit.

Suede Vest Guy leans his forehead against the edge of the window. Hugs himself and sighs. I'm crowding his personal space. I'm sure he was betting on my seat being empty. I'm going to make this whole flight miserable just with my existence.

A flight attendant's voice comes over the plane's PA system, telling us to turn off all our electronic devices.

The guy glances up at the sound of it. I can see his face for the first time. It's a kind, quiet face. His cheeks are wet with tears.

At first, I turn away. Dude, that's embarrassing.

Tracksuit woman senses something and glances at us both. When she sees the silently weeping guy in the window seat, she snaps her head back to the in-flight magazine she was reading. I can tell it's a gesture of respect. She's giving him privacy.

I'm not going to do that.

I unfold my arm and touch the guy lightly on the shoulder.

"Sir?" I say.

The guy turns to me, clearly mortified. "I'm sorry," he mutters.

"I just wanted to make sure you're all right. Are you all right?" I catch his eyes and can tell he understands what I'm really saying. *Do you need help? I can give you help.*

He wipes his cheeks and smiles a bit. "No, man. I'm not all right. But I will be." He smiles weakly and turns back to the window. I guess that's all I'm going to get of the story.

Suddenly, he turns to me again. More composed. "Thank you for asking, though. I really appreciate it."

Now he's the one to continue the conversation with a look. *You asked*, his expression says. *Not everyone would.*

I nod and turn to stare at the air vent above me. This was a small thing. Maybe I would have done it a week ago, maybe not. I want so badly to be able to talk this one out with Kendall, I feel it burning bitter in my throat.

I want so badly for Kendall to come with me on this journey, I might need that barf bag.

To hell with what she said about not contacting her.

I start typing her a message as quickly as I can. A flight attendant is already starting down the aisle, making sure everyone's devices are off.

A new character in the seat next to me, I write. **Don't know his name but I'm going to call him Hal. He's crying. When I asked him if he was okay, he said he's not but he will be. Not love, I don't think. Maybe he lost someone. Maybe his grandmother at age 100.**

I hit Send.

Come on, Kendall. If I get no reply, I'll know she's serious about not being in contact. I'll respect it completely. The flight attendant is only a few rows away now.

Come on come on come on. Just one message, and I can take off along with the aircraft I'm inside. I would have everything I need.

"Sir," comes the voice above me. "I need you to turn off your phone."

"Oops! Sorry!" I say, like I forgot I had a phone at all. Shit, she's actually going to stand there and watch me power it down. My finger goes to the button.

As it does, my phone wakes up. It vibrates and chirps.

I look down at the screen.

Someone's sent me a picture. A photo of a page full of writing. I recognize it instantly as Kendall's notebook. I see the words *Dear Luna* at the top.

My heart explodes.

And it all begins.

Acknowledgments

I'm so grateful to be able to type the words, "This is my fourth book with my editor Rosemary Brosnan." I'm also typing other words to go with those, like "amazing," "funny," "smart as hell," and simply, "she gets it." I consider myself a very lucky writer-person.

I can't imagine a better agent and friend to have as an advocate in this world than the tough, sweet, ever-savvy Jamie Weiss Chilton. She would be my number-one gym-class team pick every time.

My experience at the Kindling Words East retreat was pivotal in figuring out what I was doing with this story. Thank you, Alison James and Tanya Lee Stone, for giving writers and illustrators of children's literature this opportunity to fan the flame and reconnect with the joy of what we do.

Much appreciation to Courtney Stevenson and Jessica MacLeish of the HarperCollins crew. And yikes, Heather Daugherty! You did it again with a brilliant book cover!

Love always to the friends and family who support me unconditionally, especially Bill, Sadie, Clea, Mom, Dad, and Squash the cat. (I've never put a pet in my acknowledgments before but let me tell you, this one deserves it.)

To the readers, librarians, and teachers who have, even briefly, made my books part of their lives or work: thank you for that kindness. It's a big one for me. I hope what I write is a kindness of its own to you, in whatever form you need.